In a Dream
by
Kat Bourne

Copyright 2010

ISBN #978-0-9848178-1-8

For further information, please contact:
Theovette Publications
P.O. Box 221161
Hollywood, FL 33022
www.theovette.com

In a Dream

Dedicated to my wonderful son JJ, my family and friends.

May you, in your lifetime, reach that place where you feel fulfilled and complete.

Chapter 1

Harry Martin whistled the song "Walking on Sunshine" while taking his shower on a seemingly typical October Monday morning. He felt exhilarated as the warm water from the showerhead in the large whirlpool bathtub swiftly sprayed out and cascaded down his body. Later, before leaving his home for work that morning, Harry kissed his wife on her cheek as she looked up at him between sips of her morning cup of coffee. "Hey, Honey Bunny," he said to her. He ruffled his son Roger's hair and kissed him loudly on the cheek as Roger ate his pancakes. "Morning, Rog Dog!" he greeted. "That 'fro is growing out great!" He fist pumped his son's fist. Harry kissed his daughter Marissa's forehead as she stood drinking a cup of orange juice. "Morning, beautiful, Rissa Dissa," he said. He kissed their dear family friend and housemate Mrs. Appelbaum on the cheek while she was in the middle of chewing on a bagel with cream cheese. "Hello, gorgeous," he said to Mrs. Appelbaum. "Have a wonderful day!"

Around 7:15 a.m. when Harry exited his front door the sun was shining, the sky was a glorious azure and there wasn't a cloud in the sky. Because he resided in South Florida, birds were still present and Harry could hear them singing, squawking, cooing and chirping. Green was everywhere – in the leaves of palm, oak, fruit and other trees, as well as the grass and plants. Harry was a successful attorney, he had a wonderful wife, two great kids, good friends, and several fantastic older women and men in his life who were like surrogate parents in place of his biological, long absent parents.

Harry was dressed in a charcoal gray Armani suit purchased by his wife. Around his neck was a silk tie designed with a print of M.C. Escher's *Sky and Water* drawing – the tie was a present from Mrs. Appelbaum. After placing his leather briefcase (a birthday gift from his children) and daily newspapers in his vehicle, Harry stepped back to the porch of the family's older but contemporized 5-bedroom, 3-bathroom house. The house was tan with dark brown trim. Harry hugged and kissed his wife on the lips under a tan concrete arch built over the porch (where his wife was standing to bid him goodbye). "Love you, baby," Harry said. "Love you too, sweetie," replied his wife.

Harry felt so exultant and was in such high spirits that he was tempted to jump up and click his heels a la Gene Kelly or Fred Astaire in one of those old movies. Before entering his shiny black Ford

Explorer, he threw his car keys in the air in a carefree way, spun around and caught them successfully in his hand. He got in the driver's seat of the vehicle, blew the horn and turned on the AC. His daughter, Marissa, a freshman in high school, came running out the door with her backpack slung over one shoulder. Her hair braids flopped up and down as she ran. She was dressed in *Apple Bottom* blue jeans, a yellow short sleeve shirt with a shiny silver *Baby Phat* cat on the front, and yellow high top *Converse All Star* sneakers.

When Marissa got in the passenger seat and closed the door, Harry said, "Let's ride Clyde." As they rode Harry and Marissa sang along with Earth, Wind and Fire, "*You're a Shining Star. No matter who you are.*" When Marissa exited the Explorer at her school, she leaned over and kissed Harry on the cheek.

"Bye, Daddy," she said.

"Bye, Princess. Love you," Harry replied. Harry was in a fantastic mood.

Less than four hours later, Harry Martin was staring out the window from his 15th floor office in a dramatically different mood. He was looking through the glass, but he really wasn't seeing anything. He was in a daze; a daze that was brought on by an incident that had occurred less than fifteen minutes prior. Boy, Harry thought. It was amazing how the world and life that you were accustomed to, and which was fine the way it was, could change in an instant. A person's entire existence could be turned upside down by something as simple as a ten-minute phone call. This is what happened to Harry,

Harry felt that at any moment he was going to break down and cry. Sitting behind his shiny mahogany desk, his back cushioned by the luxuriousness of the soft leather of his chair, Harry sensed that if he didn't keep himself together, he would erupt into a bawling fit. He sniffed up the water that was beginning to drip from his nose.

He snatched up a Kleenex from the Halloween themed decorative box on his desk and held it against his nostrils. Halloween was a few weeks away and someone had given him a Kleenex container covered with ghosts and goblins.

Harry squeezed his eyes tightly to suppress the teardrops that were accumulating and threatening to gush down his face. He swallowed and breathed deeply to calm the wail that was creeping up his six-foot plus tall body. He believed if he tried to speak his words would be blocked by the lump that had become lodged in his throat. He shuddered even as the sun shone outside. Outside the weather was so calm that the leaves on the trees barely moved.

Harry's heart, body and soul felt worn out and heavy. All of this was the result of a 10 minute phone call which happened to be from the woman who had given birth to Harry; a person whom he had not seen in over 20 years. The woman who caused Harry to feel self-hatred and pain as a result of neglect, harsh, abusive language, an occasional slap across the face, and doing things such as locking him and his siblings out of the house on cold nights with no access to the bathroom because they hadn't heard her "the first time" she called them to come inside. Her actions still affected Harry to this day. She had seen her son on some Internet web page and apparently decided to phone him. Harry really wished she hadn't.

Harry could not believe the terror he felt but he just could not shake it. He had argued and won cases against some of the state's toughest litigators. Those battles were mild compared to an impending confrontation with Myrlie, his mother. His mother was not a big woman – he knew this because even when he was a kid and saw her for the last time, she wasn't much taller that he was. Now, at his current height, she probably didn't even reach his shoulders. Still, that brought him no comfort.

Harry leaned back in the black leather chair and covered his face in exasperation. He regretted ever allowing his photograph to be taken at the "Hometown Heroes Recognition Celebration," where he and others had been honored for their community work. He had been given an award for his pro bono work, which included helping indigent citizens, including people who might have been illegally evicted, immigrants (often brought to him by his and his business partner's secretaries), and other types of cases. He also mentored troubled boys and ex-convicts, doing what he could to help them get their lives moving in a positive direction. He was on the board of the Big Brothers/Big Sisters and sponsored their programs.

His own "little brother," Travis, whom he'd known for nearly twenty years, was now a doctor. Travis' mother was a drug addict, abusive and neglectful. In fifth grade, Travis began to fight, curse out teachers and skip school. Harry's mentor and friend, Chuck Gordon, found out about Travis and suggested that Harry spend time with him. At that time, Harry was a twenty-year old college student.

Harry and Travis would go to football, baseball and basketball games. They would go the movies and to the library. Harry would use some of his financial aide and salary to buy Travis new clothes. Harry was thrilled when Travis laughed out loud at Eddie Murphy clowning around in one of his movies. It had taken at least three months for Harry to crack through Travis' angry exterior. Harry was forced to put the boy in his place several times. The first time Travis crossed the line Harry looked him in the eye and said, "You're not going to talk down to me. I'm doing this because I want to, not because I have to. But you're going to have to respect me. Are we cool about that?" Travis nodded his head. "Okay," Harry said. "Let's go get some ice cream."

Travis' own "little brother," Hunter, was in college. Travis now had a wife, Justine, and a five-year-old son named Sean.

Harry felt that without the support of kind people in his own life, his world would have become a very different place. So, helping others came naturally to him. He did not participate in volunteer work for fame and recognition. He was actually surprised at the speed with which his popularity grew from his face being posted on the Internet. His face became the image associated with stories about the event, and even related accounts of people helping people. People that he hadn't seen in ages began contacting him. People that he had never met before began introducing themselves to him. Initially he was pleased and a little flattered about the attention, but several months ago a sickening feeling in his gut came over him that he couldn't place. It hit him now.

Damn, he silently cursed at the force responsible for returning this woman to his life (be it fate, coincidence or the devil, he wasn't sure). Although he hadn't heard that shrilly, loud voice in years, he knew right away who she was when she said, "Hey boo-boo," and before she said, "It's yo' mama." *What the hell does she want?* he thought. This was all he needed.

"Splittin' image of yo' daddy," she'd said. "I wa-ant always sho' who yo daddy was, but soon as I saw dat piture I knowed right den. If you ain't jes like that no good Hammer. So, you a lawya. Outa my fo' childrens I neva woulda thought you be the one makin' somethin' outa yoself. You was always kinda smart, always readin' books, but I thought you was not tough enough ta hang wit da big boys. I ain't too proud to admit it when I'm wrong.

"But anyway. Listen, Boo," she said. "Ooh, I'd love to see my baby. Yo' black self. Mama's comin' ta town and she'll be at the

4

Miami Downtown Greyhound station 'round 10 Wednesday monin'. Yo' office is 'round there somewhere, right?

"Oh, by da way, if that fii-iine chick standin' nex to you was yo' wife in one-a those pitures I saw, she sho got it goin on. Fo' sho'. Never woulda thought you had in ya' to end up wit somebody like dat, but I sho ain't mad atcha. See ya Wednesday. Don't forget – 10 o'clock at the Miami Greyhound station. Da Downtown one. Bye!" She hung up before he had a chance to blow her off or attempt to convince her that she had the wrong person.

Harry shook his head to clear his mind and regain focus. He watched a swarm of wild green parrots flying in the sky past his window. He turned his head and looked around his office. On the wood paneled wall were his Bachelor in American History and law degrees from the University of Miami; plaques and awards he received for his community work; framed drawings by his son and writings by his daughter. There were prints of paintings by Romare Bearden ("Jamming at the Savoy") and Norman Rockwell ("The Golden Rule" and "The Problem We All Live With"). A print of Pieter Bruegel's "Children's Games" also hung on the wall.

The lyrics to "Lift Every Voice and Sing" were inscribed in calligraphy on framed parchment paper bordered in shiny gold. Versions of the Preamble and Bill of Rights of the U.S Constitution; the Declaration of Independence; the Emancipation Proclamation; and Dr. Martin Luther King, Jr.'s *I Have a Dream* speech were framed on the wall. There were portraits of people that Harry admired: Dr. King, Mahatma Gandhi, Bayard Rustin, Julius Rosenwald, Grace Connors (Harry's mother-in-law, who had been lawyer, as well as a civil rights activist), Dominick Dimaio, Sr. (Harry's professional mentor and father figure) and Chuck Gordon (Harry's life mentor and good friend). There was also a photo of Harry and Claire with Denzel Washington at a Boys and Girls Club fundraising ball.

Harry looked at photos of his family on his desk. There was his wife Claire, daughter Marissa, son Roger, and the newest addition to the family: Mrs. Appelbaum, an elderly neighbor who had moved into their home after falling and breaking a hip. Harry cringed at the thought of introducing any of them to his mother. She had been married a few times by the time he was 10 so he wasn't sure what her last name was. None of the marriages lasted very long. Harry wasn't sure if she'd even gone through divorce proceedings when one marriage ended and another began. Harry was 11 when he saw her for the last time.

Harry was unsure if he would recognize Myrlie when he saw her. A slide show of fuzzy images flipped through his mind like paint swatches: Myrlie in jet black, blond, red, orange hair; in long, short and medium length wigs. There were full and wavy wigs that flowed past her shoulders, as well as pageboy and shorter styled wigs. Some hairpieces in varying lengths she used to make into ponytails. Sometimes the ponytails hung down her back like a horse's tail. In his memory, he could see her swishing along the sidewalk, deliberately tossing her head and the hairpieces. He could almost hear her high heel shoes loudly clicking against the sidewalk.

There were several occasions when he'd woken up in the middle of the night for a bathroom run, accidentally stepped on hair and freaked out because he believed he'd touched some sort of furry animal. One time he actually screamed, waking up everyone in the apartment. Myrlie called him a stupid girl and threw a shoe at him.

Harry hated when she visited his school in her short, shiny skirts and 3 or 4-inch high heels, or her favorite tight leather pants and tacky fur coat. Early in the day, her face would be made up with oily foundation, red blush on her cheeks, blue or green eye shadow and shiny red lipstick. She smelled of loud flowery perfume. She used to really embarrass him when she flirted with male teachers or even principals at school. "You married?" she'd ask.

This day in 2007 her face was almost like a blur in Harry's memory, but the bright red painted lips and gold with a star in one of her front teeth shone brightly in his mind.

Harry shook his head again. He had to get out of the office before he broke down crying the way he did as a little boy. He paged his secretary.

Rosita, a woman in her early sixties, with short, gray, neatly styled hair and soft brown eyes, stepped into Harry's office. Rosita was dressed in a red skirt and jacket suit. There was a blue silk scarf tied around her neck and she wore navy blue pumps, Rosita looked over the glasses perched on her nose and said, "Yez, Meester Marteen?"

"I'm going to step out early today," Harry said brusquely. "Got some errands I need to take care of. Cancel my appointments please."

"Shua," Rosita answered. "Will you be back in la manana?"

"Yes," Henry replied. "Probably. Let Dom know I'll fill him in later." Dom Dimaio was one of Harry's closest and longest friends. He was also Harry's business partner.

Rosita stared into his eyes for a moment. "I will see you in the morning, Mr. Marteen. I hope everything is fine."

"Yes, tomorrow," responded Harry. "Call me if an emergency comes up."

Harry grabbed his briefcase and keys and checked his watch. It was 10:47. This date and time would remain fixed in his brain. He could feel Rosita worrying behind his back. She'd been his secretary for years; was almost old enough to be his mother. Super smart lady, she'd been an attorney in her native Cuba. Harry got on the elevator.

Harry climbed into his vehicle and turned on the air. He slipped in a Billie Holiday CD and drove off. *"Am I blue,"* Billie sang in her soulful, melancholy voice. Harry decided not to go home but instead wanted to find a place to think, or a location where he wouldn't have to concentrate. He drove with no destination in mind and ultimately ended up at the mall and then near the movie theater. The theater would be nearly empty at this time of day. He could sit in the dark and cry if he wanted to. Cry – the thought sounded ridiculous. He was grown. Adult men don't cry. *Damn*, he thought again.

Harry had to wait several minutes to pay his admission at the theater counter. He quietly observed two young ladies discussing their activities over the past weekend.

"No, no you didn't," a girl with pixyish blond hair, pale white skin with freckles dotted on the nose, black lined bright green eyes and pink painted lips, said through a fit of giggles.

"Oh, yeah, I did," her dark chocolate co-worker said, twirling her long (strawberry blonde) hair weave and rolling her hazel colored eyes, which Harry was sure were contact lenses. There was a pinkish shade of eye shadow on her eyelids. Her full lips were painted a glossy burgundy. She had on foundation that appeared to be a few shades lighter than on her own skin.

"No, no way," the pale girl answered. "Oh, my God!" Then her head fell back and she broke into a hyena-like laugh.

"Yeah---I did!" the dark girl answered. Then she flipped her hair, grinned and turned toward Harry.

"Welcome to AMC. How may I help you?"

7

"One for *Michael Clayton*," Harry said. He paid and as he walked away, he took one last look at the girls. The pale one was still laughing - her head face down on the counter in front of her and her body convulsing. The dark one was still twirling her weave and rocking her body to a song Harry could not hear.

A Coca-Cola commercial was just ending when Harry entered the theater. The previews began following the commercial. A couple of Harry's gym buddies had seen *Michael Clayton*. He'd heard that George Clooney played this lawyer who could get folks out of bad situations. If Myrlie were that same irritating person, her arrival would be nothing more than a horrible situation. A situation Michael Clayton or a hit man (he joked to himself) might have been able to resolve.

Funny, but George Clooney actually resembled one of his mother's old boyfriends. Harry tried to remember the guy's name but couldn't. The guy had this way of making Harry and his brothers laugh. He'd fake punch the wall pretending to hurt his hand, or do the down elevator trick behind the couch. The man's face was hazy, but his gray hair stood out in Harry's memory because he wasn't a senior citizen – he was what they call prematurely gray. He was that smooth kind of white guy like Clooney. Harry had to acknowledge that with all her faults, his mom certainly didn't discriminate.

There was a succession of men. Harry couldn't place their faces or most of the names, but shapes, sizes and color variations filled his mind. There were dark white men with dark hair, pale white men with blond ponytails, bald men, dark black men, light black men. There were fat men, skinny men, tall men and short men.

One man must have been a midget or dwarf because when Harry opened the bathroom door early one morning he stood face to face with a man his height; the man's fat stomach touching Harry's. Harry was about 8 years old. He felt very strange staring straight into the bloodshot eyes of this guy with the bushy eyebrows and moustache that curled at the tips. Harry was close enough to smell strong liquor on the man's breath. When Harry stepped back to get some space, he noticed that his mother's friend was wearing a baseball cap with a bunny and the words "PLAYBOY" imprinted on it. His gray t-shirt read "I ROCK WITH JESUS." Apparently, the midget had just gotten dressed to leave because a few minutes later Harry heard the front door open and close.

Now, at the movie theater Harry settled into his seat and watched the previews. The movie began several minutes later. Harry tried to calculate his strategy for the coming days. There were hundreds of things he'd rather do than introduce Myrlie to his family, like jump out of a speeding car, he thought; or eat nails. Trying to find humor in the situation did not ease the queasiness he felt in his stomach.

Harry and his wife had gone through a difficult couple of years. They had been separated for over a year and were starting to get things back on track. The Myrlie he remembered most certainly would not bring anything positive to the situation. His instincts told him that she'd bring nothing but trouble.

Even though he was unable to fully focus on the movie plot line and dialogue, and wasn't sure how much of the movie had played while he had been distracted, Harry was now watching a tormented attorney wrestle with some kind of internal demons on the movie screen. It wasn't George Clooney but an older man. Anguish was convincingly portrayed on the actor's face. Harry wanted to show the opposite. When he stepped out of the movie theater he hoped his facial expression would not reveal the hate, fear and misery he was currently feeling.

In the darkness of the movie theater Harry closed his eyes. Images of his difficult childhood started appearing before his shut eyelids. Incidents he'd tried to forget through the years flashed through his mind like short movies or TV clips.

Harry's mind drifted back some twenty something years. In blurry scenes playing in his mind, he was seeing Myrlie's contorted face. He was hearing in his head Myrlie's harsh angry words: *You ugly loser! You black punk! Ain't go'n never amount to nothin'. None of y'all.* When one of them wet the bed, she'd yell loud enough for the whole neighborhood to hear: "Should make you wear those pissy draws for a coupla days! See if that make you stop wettin' up my sheets!"

He was remembering how she'd disappear for days and days, leaving them with no food and money. He and his brothers would go out after school and work odd jobs to earn money for food and hygiene necessities such as toilet tissue and toothpaste. On days when they skipped school, they would wait until they saw other kids walking with schoolbooks in the afternoon. Then they would do their errands or odd jobs. There might be a few old ladies who needed someone to run to the store; a barber who'd pay a couple of dollars to get his shop swept up; someone who needed snow shoveled during the winter - things like that.

Sometimes his brother Billy shoplifted food and other items. He had not seen Billy, nor his other brother Lenny or his sister Lucy in years.

On the day that changed his life forever Harry and his siblings were sitting in a back bedroom in one of the many apartments where they'd lived. They had missed several days of school. Their mom had disappeared again. Fortunately, this time she'd stocked up the refrigerator and cabinets with food, so they weren't starving. The family had recently gone shopping with the thick stack of food stamps Myrlie had received earlier in the week. There had been times when she left them without food. There were times when she left and neglected to pay the light bill. Harry became accustomed to sitting in dark rooms. He became accustomed to not having a cooked or any meal every day.

Harry couldn't remember why they were not attending school that day when his world was transformed, but he did recall that people had started coming around banging on the door. Harry and his siblings were terrified that they were going to be taken away. Their instincts were correct.

Harry silently sobbed in the blackness. Warm tears slid slowly down his cheeks. He wiped them away with a wadded up tissue that had been gripped in his hand.

Harry had fallen asleep. When he woke up and looked around more seats had been filled. He checked the time on his cell phone and realized that it was almost 4:30 p.m. His movie had started at 12 so the film had probably played a few times. Work usually prevented him from rarely arriving home before 6:00 p.m.. He didn't mind being home before sunset but this day he had to compose himself. He had to practice his happy face. He wasn't ready to discuss Myrlie; not even with his wife.

He got up, washed his face in the theater bathroom, exited the theater, and stepped out into the mall. Even though "malling" was of one his least favorite activities he decided to check out the place. His wife, daughter and Mrs. Appelbaum loved what they called "malling." Marissa and her friends behaved as if going to the mall was a special occasion. Harry had overheard Marissa's telephone conversations in which she agonized over what she was going to wear to the mall.

Harry didn't understand the females' fascination with the place – he hated the crowds and thought the stores overflowing with clothes were obscene. However, the women in his life had no problem spending hours and hours at the mall. Even Mrs. Appelbaum, who was in her 80's, had unbelievable stamina for "malling."

This Monday afternoon's mall crowd included some senior citizens, mothers with smaller children, and older kids who had probably arrived after school. Harry was thankful that the mall wasn't filled to the brim with bodies. He was able to walk freely without sidestepping or crashing into other shoppers.

Harry window-shopped a bit and checked out some fancy gadgets in an electronic store. He bought several CDs at a record store. He purchased a *LEGO Star Wars* toy that he and his son could work on together – Roger enjoyed building things with blocks. Then Harry sat down to eat at the food court. He was able to stretch out the time and when he checked his watch and noted that it was after 6:00 p.m. he decided to go on home. Outside the sun was going down and the sky was getting darker. Orange-red jagged lines striped across the horizon.

As he drove home Harry listened to Gary Wright's song "Dreamweaver," one of his favorite tunes. Then he inserted a Bob James CD to hear smooth jazz piano. Harry agonized over how he would make it through the evening, through the upcoming days. In the final minutes of his ride home Harry listened to "Remember to Breath" by Marcus Cole. *Breathe, breathe, breathe,* thought Harry. Harry took a deep breath upon entering the driveway of his home. He double-checked his face to make sure there were no dried tears streaked along his face. He squirted Visine in his eyes. Then he exhaled.

Chapter 2

Sometimes Claire Martin felt twangs of guilt about the way she treated her husband during the year following her mother's death. There were times when she even felt remorse about her behavior towards him when they were college students.

Claire couldn't place the moment when Harry became a fixture in her life. They were both attending law school at the University of Miami and at some point, it became apparent to her that Harry was almost like a shadow, following her around like a little puppy. She actually had a boyfriend at the time, Craig, who was the classic, cool, handsome, football jock. She and Craig had dated since high school and by the time she met Harry, Craig had become a professional football player. With Craig, there was always a sense that he was never being completely honest. She would discover that he had been hanging out with girls and then he'd swear he and the girl were just friends. The females would tell a different story. Claire fell for Craig's version more than once.

Harry was a different kind of man. After becoming friends, Claire and Harry would "hang out." Early in the friendship they would spend time together; frankly, when Claire had nothing else to do. Harry would make or buy her favorite foods if she was depressed; for special occasions; or just to make sure she had something to eat. She often stood him up when a better offer came in the form of a big party; or a group getting together for a football game; or dancing at a nightclub; or maybe to go out with Craig.

Harry began inviting her to functions and places where he had previously gone alone. They went to jazz and classical music concerts. They went to video arcades – Harry could completely engage himself in *Mario, Donkey Kong, Galaga or Tron.* They went to Star Trek Conventions (many strange people attended those) and Renaissance Festivals. Harry revealed to her that before she came along he would just peruse the different exhibits and events, not having very much involvement at all. Surprising even herself, Claire spontaneously suggested that they wear costumes to one of the functions. Even though she felt a little goofy, she thought they might as well *really* participate. Choosing, buying and wearing costumes was a habit that stayed and she actually grew to enjoy it. She would feel almost embarrassed at the excitement and pride that would be in Harry's eyes when they strolled through the venues. Claire would dare her roommate Sharon to laugh when she entered the living room wearing one of the medieval maiden dresses, Princess Leia or Lieutenant Uhuru costumes. Sharon would just smile and shake her head.

One weekend Claire and Harry spent nearly a full Saturday and Sunday in a movie theater at an Alfred Hitchcock movie festival. *Psycho, Vertigo, The Birds* and *Rear Window* were some of the films that were shown. The original *Star Wars* movie had been re-released one year and was shown on movie screens throughout the country. Claire watched the entire movie for the first time with Harry. Harry loved the films *Brian's Song* and *Willy Wonka and the Chocolate Factory*. Claire watched them several times with him. Harry knew the lyrics to the songs in *Wonka*. His favorites were "Pure Imagination" and "Cheer Up, Charlie." He was very shy, however, when Claire heard him sing. Some of Harry's other movie favorites were *Shawshank Redemption, Glory, Ferris Bueller's Day Off, A Soldier's Story, A Raisin in the Sun*, the *Back to the Future* series, the *Indiana Jones* movies, *Carmen Jones, The Heart is a Lonely Hunter, To Kill a Mockingbird, Marty* and *Forrest Gump*. Harry was a *Batman* fan (the old TV show and movies). Claire was just a little surprised to learn that Harry was a major fan of the *Color Purple* (the book and movie).

During the friendship, and later, dating phases, Harry and Claire would stargaze on the beach using Harry's telescope. Harry would point out constellations to Claire. Harry would sometimes read from Ralph Ellison's *Invisible Man* (of which he owned a treasured first edition). He read from Charles Dickens', Alexandre Dumas' and Mark Twain's novels. He and Claire had several discussions about the character Jim the slave in *The Adventures of Huckleberry Finn*. Claire had a problem with Twain's use of the word nigger. Harry said when the book was published the word was part of the culture and language. He pointed out that Huck learned to see Jim as a person – as a man and not just a slave. Harry owned a first edition copy of *Catcher in the Rye*. He said that he could relate to Holden Caulfield. One of Harry's favorite books was Jean Toomer's *Cane*. He liked novels by Tolstoy and Flannery O'Connor.

Harry turned Claire on to the show *Quantum Leap* in which scientist Sam "leaped" or traveled back in time and entered another person's body. Sam became aware of his mission after he was unexpectedly transported to the past and into someone else's life and problems.

Even though it sounded cliqueish, Claire really did think of Harry as just a friend – for a long time. She always thought he was very attractive with his dark brown chocolaty skin, smooth full lips, dazzling smile, and dreamy eyes, but he was rather nerdy. He preferred to wear inexpensive, pullover, patterned sweaters or long sleeved shirts buttoned up to the neck. His shirts were always tucked in his pants. He rarely wore jeans. Although it pained her to admit it, she was bothered by the fact that Harry was a poor, simple man. Nothing like Craig or the other guys she was used to dating. Although Craig was a cheater and a liar, he had an outgoing personality and was handsome and smooth. Claire enjoyed the frills of being a football player's girlfriend. There were exciting parties with fancy hor dourves, champagne, movie stars and famous sports celebrities. She'd even attended a few red carpet movie premiers and award shows with Craig.

Her mother turned up her nose at all that stuff. "Those big time people aren't any better than you and me," Mrs. Connors would say. Mrs. Connors appreciated Harry immediately. Claire would fume with silent anger when she discovered that Harry had taken a trip to Atlanta to assist her mother in some way. "My, my, my, that Harry is one wonderful man," her mother would brag. "He drove all the way here to make sure I was okay after that bad storm."

"Claire, he's crazy about you," her mother would say. "Don't let him get away. He's nice, tall, dark and handsome. He reminds me of Richard Roundtree, the actor who played Shaft. He may not be smooth as Craig, or some of those other ones, but I don't think Craig is the right man for you. How many times have you caught Craig with another chick? I'm tired of seeing you crying over that guy. Harry loves you. In my gut, I know Harry is the perfect man for you. I just know it."

"Well, you date him!" Claire snapped back. Harry sat with Claire while she cried her heart out after breaking up with Craig. Craig shrugged his shoulders and found a new girlfriend the following week. He had probably been seeing the woman the whole time.

Harry stayed around when she began dating other popular, wealthy men. There were more professional football *and* basketball players. Claire would use that old Marcia Brady line, "something came up," to explain herself when she cancelled plans with Harry. She couldn't pinpoint the exact date and time when she'd find herself waiting for Harry to call, or when her heart would ache when he'd be gone off somewhere and she didn't see him for days. She couldn't say for sure when it was that her heart began to dance when Harry appeared; when she stopped trying to fix him up with other women; and when she began to feel sick with jealousy when she'd see him with someone else. There came a time when Claire felt a tingle in her whole body anytime Harry flashed his white teeth in his wide, gorgeous smile or stared at her with his dark, dreamy brown eyes.

One rainy Saturday they spent most of the entire day in Harry's apartment. That day Harry read Oscar Wilde's *The Happy Prince* to her. He read poetry including works by Tennyson and Walt Wiltman. He played jazz and classical music. One of his favorite pieces was "Clair de Lune" by Debussy. He cooked lunch and dinner for her. They watched Jimmy Stewart in *Harvey* and *It's a Wonderful Life*. Claire had never watched *It's a Wonderful Life*. It touched her when George Bailey's friends came to support him at the end. That woman Mary loved George Bailey with all her heart. Together, they watched Claire's ultimate guilty pleasure movie, *Dirty Dancing*.

Claire thought, *This man, Harry, is one of a kind.* She turned off the TV and took Harry's hand. She escorted him to his bedroom, unbuttoned and removed his shirt and removed his pants. She kissed him and said, "I love you, Harry." That day was the first time they made love. She had "accidentally" kissed him before when she was still with Craig. Her heart twitched even then but she ignored it.

Every few years, Claire would get pangs of regret for the times she mistreated Harry. Harry turned out to be the kindest man she'd ever met, with the exception of her father. She cringed at the thought that she'd almost run him away for good more than once. He was gone for over a year after she virtually threw him out of the house shortly after her mother passed away.

Claire's mother had been ill with cancer for several years. When it became obvious that she should not live alone, they invited her to move from Georgia and into their home in Florida. It was difficult for Claire to witness the toll the cancer and medications had taken on her mother. Claire's mother's hair became very thin and brittle; she lost a lot of weight; and her smooth, brown skin began to feel papery and dry. Even though her mother's body had become weaker, Claire was still unprepared for the shock of seeing her lifeless body one morning. Claire had lain down beside her mother that previous evening for hours. She thought she'd have some kind of warning when her mother passed away, but when it happened unexpectedly, she lost it. She began yelling and howling, "No, no, no! Mama, mama! Wake up! Please, Mama, please wake up. Oh, God, No!" Her children came running into the room. They tried to comfort her. As she cried, little Roger put his arms around her shoulder and Marissa held her hands.

A few months after that day, Claire began to lash out at Harry, taking out all her anger and pain on him. Everything he said or did was wrong. Thinking about some of the vicious words hurled at Harry from her lips caused her stomach to tighten up.

"You're probably glad she's dead! You really didn't want her here anyway!" She knew even then that the accusations were false but she couldn't stop.

"Leave me alone!" she shouted. "I need some goddamn space from you!" One morning, Harry packed a bag and with tears in his eyes, quietly left the house.

After they separated, she would make outrageous accusations. When he would arrive to take his children out for the weekend, she would accuse him of attempting to kidnap them. "What took you so long to get back with my children? I was getting ready to call the police." She shuddered at the ridiculousness of those statements. He didn't even argue back with her. He started communicating with *his* children by telephone.

He wanted to continue paying all of the bills. She allowed him to pay the mortgage and her car payment. She took a waitress job at a place called *Pete's Grill* to pay the remaining bills.

Claire's daughter, Marissa, hated Claire for a long time after that, especially during Christmas. Harry allowed Claire to handle Christmas 2005 alone because he didn't want it to appear as if they were competing. He didn't want to make Claire look inadequate. Marissa was not happy with the inexpensive gifts she received. That year Marissa did not receive expensive designer brand clothing. She got a *Walkman* instead of an *iPod*. Marissa was not pleased at all. Roger missed his father but as far as Christmas, he was fine with the *Lego's,* clothing and action figures that he received.

Claire shook her head. She could not believe some of the things that came out of her mouth back then. Thank God, Harry was the man he was because if he had not continued to support her and the children financially, she's not sure what would have happened.

When Harry had left this particular morning in 2007, he seemed to be on top of the world. For dinner the night before the family had eaten black beans and rice and made tacos together. Roger, their ten-year-old son, had the ingenious idea to add Skittles and marshmallows to a taco.

"Yuck! Ugh!" he groaned, when he took a bite into the concoction. "This is nasty!"

Apparently the new taco recipe wasn't as delicious as he'd imagined. Chewed up Skittles, marshmallows, ground beef, tomatoes and lettuce ended up in a glob on his plate. Fourteen year old Marissa gagged and said, "Ooh, that's gross! You so stupid, Boy!" Mrs. Appelbaum, Claire and Harry laughed hysterically. Afterwards, they all played a game of Monopoly. It was really a pleasant night.

However, today, when Harry walked into the dining room, his shoulders were slumped over and even though he tried to hide it, Claire noticed that the tortured look she had witnessed over the years had returned to his eyes. This wasn't the first time when Harry's mood had changed within hours, but this Monday he seemed more down than usual. Claire was worried. Something had upset him. She wondered if something from his past had crept up on him.

Harry's childhood was a mystery to Claire. She had never met his mother or anyone else in his family. She'd been tempted to dissolve her marriage on the grounds of secrecy but Harry was a fantastic father and husband. She had broached the subject throughout the years and ceased when she witnessed the overwhelming sadness and a bit of fear in her husband's eyes. Her instincts told her that he would talk when he was ready. She couldn't imagine what he'd been through.

Claire had never known Harry to shout or even use hostile language, except maybe when he was trying a case in court or when someone threatened his family. He had never raised his hand to her or their children. But there were times in the middle of the night when he'd wake up shaking. Those times Claire knew he wouldn't want to talk so she'd just hold him tight.

Her own childhood had been wonderful. She had been a spoiled only child. All she had to do was request anything and she got it, especially from her father. He thought she could do no wrong and could not bring himself to discipline her. Punishment fell to Claire's mother who had delivered several strong words to Claire throughout the years.

By the time Claire was 14 she had grown taller than both of her parents, eventually reaching 5'9". Her father was around 5'4" or 5'5" and weighed no more than 150 pounds. Her mother was about 2 inches shorter than he was. People would say, "Ain't they the cutest couple." A girl couldn't wish for better parents.

Claire would watch her father staring at her mother as if she was an expensive piece of art or a fancy car. Her parents held hands when they walked in public. They would stroll together with Claire in the middle, Claire holding one of each of their hands. Their many trips to Disney World were like fantasy vacations. Her father loved going on all the rides with her.

When her father arrived home from work, he would slip kisses on both their cheeks while her mother cooked dinner and Claire did her homework. He would chop vegetables and help out in many other ways. When things needed to be repaired he'd make sure they were done right away. Her mother sat nestled next to her father when they watched detectives Barnaby Jones, Kojak, Jim Rockford and other TV favorites. They'd crack up over the antics of Fred Sanford, Archie Bunker, JJ Evans, George Jefferson and Carol Burnett and her costars. Something about Bob Newhart's deadpan humor when he portrayed a psychologist made her father laugh uproariously.

The three of them enjoyed watching *Diff'rent Strokes*. Laughing, Claire's dad would repeat *"What you talkin' 'bout Willis"*. Oh, how Claire missed her father's deep, loud laugh. Claire sometimes joined her mother to watch *Golden Girls, Amen, In the Heat of the Night, Murder She Wrote* and *Dynasty* after Mr. Connors' death.

Claire liked seeing wisecracking Dee on *What's Happenin'*. Claire wore funky clothes and changed her hair several times to resemble *The Cosby Show's* Denise Huxtable. Her mother would say, "Girl, what have you done to your hair?" *Wonder Woman, Facts of Life, A Different World, Living Single, 227, South Central,* the CW's *The Game, Bernie Mac Show, Sex and The City, Girlfriends* and *Dawson's Creek* were on the list of Claire's favorite shows. She discovered

Dawson's after it was cancelled, began watching reruns and became addicted to the show. Claire would laugh so hysterically watching *Martin* that tears would come to her eyes. Back in the day, she would swoon when Blair Underwood appeared on screen in *LA Law*. She had crushes on Todd Bridges, as well as the guys in New Edition and New Kids on the Block. Claire was still loyal to New Edition, having purchased all of their albums. In 2005, New Edition went on their first tour in years. Claire and Harry were separated at the time. She felt strange going without Harry - her pride prevented her from inviting him so she did not go to the show. She later regretted her decision.

Claire was one of Will Smith's most dedicated fans, owning all of his movies on DVD, the *Fresh Prince of Bel Air* series DVD collection and all of Will's Smith's albums. Both she and Harry admired Will for his humanitarian work. A more re recent celebrity crush Claire had developed was Idris Alba a/k/a Stringer Bell of *TheWire.*

Claire was a fan of Bruce Willis (*Diehard*), Tom Cruise (*Top Gun)*, Eddie Murphy (*Beverly Hills Cop* and *Nutty Professor),* Matt Damon (*Bourne Identity* series*)* and the movies *Goodfellas, Love Jones, Dirty Dancing, Soul Food* and *Love and Basketball.* She did not support drug dealing but found Wesley Snipes in his colorful suits appealing as kingpins in *Sugar Hill* and *New Jack City*

Harry was far from being a jealous, possessive kind of man. However, when he joked about Claire's admiration for male celebrities, Claire pointed out Harry's own celebrity crushes: Nia Long, Halle Berry, Meryl Streep, Gabriela Montero, Janet Jackson and Madonna. On her first visit to Harry's his apartment, Claire noticed pictures of Janet posted on Harry's wall, including the one from the *Control* album cover, as well as a picture of Madonna on her *True Blue* album cover. Every now and then Claire would also bring out Harry's plastic protected *Sports Illustrated* magazine with Tyra Banks as the first black woman on the cover. He thought that Naomi Campbell was a goddess.

In fairness to Harry, he was a history buff who owned many pieces of historical memorabilia including newspapers and magazines on the downing of the Twin Towers, Hurricane Andrew and the ending of the Cold War. He had material on Nelson Mandela's release from prison and the abolishment of South Africa's apartheid. His large magazine collection included the 60th anniversary edition of *Ebony* with Oscar winners, Halle Berry, Denzel Washington and Jamie Foxx on the cover. Harry also possessed original newspapers he had found regarding the moon landing, as well as the assassinations of Martin Luther King, Jr. and President John F. Kennedy.

The Connors had loved listening to music: Claire and her mother took turns dancing with her father. He called them "my two girls." There were moments when her parents assumed that Claire had fallen asleep, but she would be quietly watching them dance to their own music. They'd play Dinah Washington's "My Funny Valentine," Frank Sinatra's "Blue Moon," the Inkspots and Ella Fitzgerald's "I'm Beginning to See the Light," and Nancy Wilson's "The Very Thought of You" over and over. Those songs became favorites of Claire and Harry's.

Over many card games of Scrabble, Monopoly or card games, Claire's father would say, "At first I thought I didn't have a chance. I used to think, *What would this classy, smart, beautiful brown skinned lady want with a dried up, yellow, slow-minded, rusty Navy man mechanic?* Me, Joe Connors. With a lawyer? A pretty lawyer at that! Can't believe how lucky I am to have the two of you." Then he would shake his head as if he really couldn't believe it.

"My mama didn't raise no fool," her mother would respond. "Claire, your daddy is the best and smartest man in the world. Good looking, too. Look at him, with his handsome self. Oh, but you already know all this. Look at what we made together – you, Claire. The most beautiful girl in the world! It would've been the worst mistake in my life to let some other woman get her hands on this trillion dollar prize.

"I was 32 years old when I met this wonderful man. I'm glad I didn't let folks convince me I was some kind of old maid and talk me into marrying some other guy who would've never loved me like this. This man right here is my prince charming. People tried to tell me this wouldn't work because he's a mechanic and I'm a lawyer. Thank goodness I was too smart to listen to that mess. You know he had a girlfriend when we met, don't you? I felt bad for that other lady but I fell in love with this guy the first time I laid eyes on him. I could just sense the kindness and gentleness in his spirit. And the way he really listened when I talked to him - Well, that just sealed the deal."

Her father would blush and his eyes would mist.

Her father's death when she was 19 devastated Claire. She had gone out to a football game and several parties after the game. When she returned there was a note on her bed to contact her mother at a local hotel. She figured that her parents had flown in together; so she waited until the next morning and went over the hotel. When she knocked on the hotel room door, one of her mother's friends, Ms. Clara, opened the door. Claire's mother was lying on the bed – her eyes were puffy and red.

Claire nervously questioned them. Her mother seemed very distraught. "Where's Daddy?" Claire asked. "Is he sick or something? Do you need me to leave school to go to the hospital?"

When Ms. Clara squeezed her shoulder and said softly, "I'm sorry, baby," Claire lost it.

"Mama!" Claire screamed. "Is Daddy in the hospital? I want my daddy! I want my daddy!" she yelled.

Claire heard fragments of sentences coming from Ms. Clara's lips - "heart attack" - "passed away" - "flew in" - "tell you" – "in person" and then Claire blacked out. She wouldn't eat for a week. After the funeral, her mother insisted she return to school, saying that her father would not want her to lose time in school. In the days that followed Claire cried many times on her roommate Sharon's and her boyfriend Craig's shoulders. (Craig did have his good points). Some days, even now, the ache of missing per parents would grip Claire's heart and soul making it difficult for her to breathe.

When Harry arrived that evening, the family had already eaten dinner. Marissa was in her bedroom. Roger was in the den playing video games with his friend Tommy. Mrs. Appelbaum was at the dining table sorting jewelry that they planned on redesigning and selling at the store they'd opened nearly two years ago: *Applemar Jewelry and Things*. Claire was typing into her laptop, handling administrative and accounting work for the store. She stopped when Harry walked in looking exhausted and defeated.

Chapter 3

"Hey, Honey!" Harry greeted Claire in an unsuccessful attempt at a light, breezy tone. "How you doing Mrs. Appelbaum?" He kissed both of them on the cheek. He didn't eat dinner, only drank a glass of water. He went to their bedroom, took off his shoes, suit and button down shirt. He pulled on a pair of pajama pants. In the pants, a t-shirt and socks he flopped down on top of the tropical themed king size bed comforter (it was designed with pictures of bird of paradise plants, banana leaves, palm trees, and blue crocus flowers). Shortly thereafter, Harry closed his eyes and fell asleep.

He dreamed that an oversized white dove was carrying him across the ocean. The bird gently placed him on an isolated tropical island with palm trees, green plants and colorful flowers. Claire was holding out her hand to him while the bird, perched on a tree, watched over him as if he were one of her children.

When Harry woke up it was the following morning.

Chapter 4

Harry was asleep when Claire went in to question him. It wasn't eight yet but because it was October and autumn darkness had fallen over the sky.

Often he brought home material to review for his cases and every single night he checked in with the kids. This night he did none of those things. Retiring early to bed was never part of his schedule. When Claire saw him curled up on top of the covers he appeared to be in a peaceful state. She didn't have the heart to disrupt his sleep. Instead she covered him with a soft blanket.

Then she joined Mrs. Appelbaum, Marissa, Roger and Kristin (a friend of Marissa's), who were all now in the den, watching television while taking apart jewelry pieces. Claire watched her son who was wearing a *Spiderman* t-shirt, seriously and diligently removing beautiful glass beads from a broken antique necklace. She often joked that Roger was confident in his masculinity. He designed lovely pieces. *That's my baby* she thought.

Roger was growing his hair out and now had an Afro that was about 3 inches long. His complexion was about the color of a Hershey's chocolate bar. His eyes were the color of maple syrup and appeared to have the fluidity of maple syrup. His eyelashes were long and thick. He was thin and when he smiled, he had dimples and the two big teeth of a ten year old. He curled his bottom lip under his teeth when he was focused on something.

Roger was definitely a mama's boy. At ten, he still sometimes cuddled next to Claire when they watched television. Roger liked to clown around. It never surprised Claire and Harry when they received phone calls from his teachers during the first few months of each school year. "He's a wonderful, kind, generous boy, a good student," the teachers would say. "He's just a little talkative." Claire would never admit this to most people, but they would get him to settle down with bribes: promises of video games and toys that he had requested.

Roger was very artistic. He had won several prizes including a bicycle, cash and savings bonds for his drawings and paintings. As Claire looked at her children this evening, she was tempted to take them in her arms and kiss them all over their faces. She loved her children so much. She refrained from the smooches. Everyone was a busy at work.

"Mama, what's up with Daddy?" Marissa asked. "He didn't even come to say hey or nothin'. He didn't ask me how my day was at school like he usually does. He's sleepin' already. I don't get that."

"Yeah," said Roger. "I wanted to see if he could help me with my math homework. I was whippin' Tommy's butt in *Madden*. Daddy shoulda seen me. Maybe I should try to wake him up."

"No," Claire answered. "Let him rest a little bit."

"Yes, we will let Harry rest tonight," said Mrs. Appelbaum. *Dancing with the Stars* will be on it a moment. Julianne, Edyta and Cheryl are adorable girls. Maxsim and Mel are fabulous. My husband Carl, bless his soul, and I have seen Wayne Newton perform in Las Vegas. Wayne is still a very charming man." Mrs. Appelbaum did a little chair dance and snapped her fingers.

"All right," answered Claire. "Let's watch *Dancing with the Stars*. Kristin, do you need me to take you home?"

"Can she say the night?" asked Marissa "She can wear some of my clothes to school tomorrow. We already checked with her mama."

"Okay," answered Claire. She sat down to join them. Inwardly she was very worried about her husband.

Chapter 5

When Harry opened his eyes Tuesday morning, Claire was sitting in the rocking chair they had purchased before Marissa's birth. Her face was turned toward the window. Sunlight streamed into the room and lit on Claire. Harry thought she looked like an angel.

Harry wished he could remain asleep for hours and days. Then when he awoke, Myrlie would have come and gone. *Wouldn't it be nice,* he thought, *if there was a fast forward button for life?* If there were such a thing Myrlie's visit would be a past memory. In that future, the dread that was causing tangled knots in his gut would be untied and he would be free again.

Indecision unsettled him. He didn't know if he should take off from work and stay home. If he went to work he could give his secretary the day off, shut his door and spend the day locked away handling legal work. However, even if he gave his secretary the day off, his partner Dom would surely question him. If he stayed home, Claire would hang around to confront him. He would be forced to deal with this crisis – Myrlie, the traveling tornado.

Claire must have heard him move because she turned around and then she spoke to him.

"Okay, Harry," Claire said. "What's going on? I'm worried about you, the kids are worried about you, and Mrs. Appelbaum is worried. You coming down with something? Your eyes were red and puffy when you came in last night; like you'd been crying or something. You didn't seem to be yourself.

"The kids have left for school," Claire said. "I called Delilah and she's going to open up the shop. Mrs. Appelbaum and I didn't want to leave until we made sure you were okay. So, tell me, honey. I'm your wife. I'm supposed to be your best friend. Talk to me, please."

Harry opened his mouth to speak, but unexpectedly he began sobbing and couldn't stop. He sat up, brought his knees up to his chest and hid his face. His body was shaking.

Claire pulled the rocking chair closer to the bed and leaned close to her husband.

"Oh, baby, baby, what's wrong? What's wrong?" she asked. Harry felt weak. He felt less than a man, but he still was unable to stop the sobbing that was ransacking his body. Claire got out of the rocking chair and sat in front of Harry on the bed. She gently lifted up his head and wiped his tears with her fingers. Then she grabbed some tissue from her nightstand and wiped his nose. She held his hands and looked in his eyes. He blinked but managed to look at her.

"Okay, listen, honey. First, I'm gonna call Rosita and tell her you're not coming in today and possibly tomorrow or even the next day. Give her a couple of days off with pay, if that's okay with you. If she wants to come in, that'll be up to her. We'll decide what you want to tell Dom. I'm sure he'll back you up.

'Then, I'm going to drop Mrs. Appelbaum off at the store. She, Delilah and Nora can handle things for one day. Mrs. Appelbaum taught me everything I know, so the store will be in excellent hands. Then I'm coming right back here and we will talk. Okay, sweetheart.

She tenderly kissed his lips and wiped away more tears.

"I love you. You know that, don't you?" she said softly. "You're gorgeous, sensitive, and brilliant. A magnificent husband and father. When my mama got sick you drove all the way to Georgia and helped her clear out her house and then brought her back here. You allowed her to live here and helped me take care of her. She would brag about all the times you sat there by her bedside until she fell asleep. I know you loved her. When Mrs. Appelbaum broke her hip and we knew she could not live alone anymore, you didn't hesitate to make her feel comfortable moving into our home. You treated my mama and you treat Mrs. Appelbaum like a real man would treat his own mother. You treat me like I'm some kind of goddess, which I'm sure I don't deserve. I thank God every day that you never gave up on me even when I was being a snobbish, ignant bitch and I know sometimes I was. Thank you." She kissed him. "Thank you." She kissed him again. "Thank you."

She stood up. "Now I have to calm down that old Jewish lady. She's gonna have to make sure you're all right. She'll be sick all day if she can't see for herself. Hey, Mrs. Appelbaum!"

"I will be right there," Mrs. Appelbaum answered. Minutes later, Mrs. Appelbaum, dressed in a torquoise pantsuit with yellow sunflowers, was standing in the bedroom doorway. Her hair was in the bun she wore daily. Her *Joy* perfume and Claire's *Chanel Coco Mademoiselle* sweetened the room. Harry held out his hand to Mrs. Appelbaum. She walked in, gently squeezed his hand and kissed his forehead. "We love you," said Mrs. Appelbaum.

"I'll see you when I get back," Claire said. She grabbed her Coach purse and said, "Let's go Mrs. Appelbaum."

Chapter 6

Mrs. Appelbaum wouldn't stop talking.

"Oh, my, my, my. I am so worried. What is wrong with our Harry? What is wrong with our Harry? He look so sad when he come home. He is usually up and about early in the morning, laughing or singing. Oh, Claire, dahling, what is wrong with our wonderful Harry."

"I don't know Mrs. Appelbaum," Claire answered. "I'm worried, too. He takes great care of all of us but keeps all of his worries all bottled of inside of him. As soon as I drop you off I'm gonna go him to talk." Tears were filling Claire's eyes and her voice was breaking. "I'm gonna get him to talk, Mrs. Appelbaum. I don't know what happened to him when he was a boy, but sometimes I believe there are demons in his past that come back to haunt him."

"Yes, yes, yes, Mrs. Appelbaum responded. "I am one who knows how much a painful past can harm a person. Ah, here we are at the store. My, my, my, what is wrong with our Harry?"

Appelmar Jewelry and Things sold handmade as well as new manufactured jewelry. Some pieces were costume and some were 10, 14 and 18-karat gold and Sterling Silver.

Mrs. Appelbaum had been an art student in her native country and was in the second year of her studies when the Nazis came rushing through her town. She related that before her family was taken into captivity, many of their friends' businesses had been burned or looted. She said that she was not sure what became of her parents, brother and sister, but believed that they had died.

Mrs. Appelbaum and her husband, Carl, had owned and operated a jewelry store for many years. They had been married for over 50 years and had no children. When Carl died in his sleep one night after they had enjoyed a night of dancing on Miami Beach, she felt that she was all alone again. Afterwards, she began filling up her days with several classes at a senior center.

Claire and Roger had met Mrs. Appelbaum one morning as they were walking to the park. After that meeting they would have cordial conversations and later became acquaintances. When Mrs. Appelbaum was ill Claire would drop by her home to bring breakfast or chicken soup. Other times Claire would play Mrs. Appelbaum's piano. Roger enjoyed black and white cookies that Mrs. Appelbaum made. Roger watched television while Claire and Mrs. Appelbaum talked.

The relationship between Mrs. Appelbaum and the Martins became even stronger in early 2006 when Marissa offered to help Mrs. Appelbaum carry grocery bags on a windy day. Following that day, Marissa and Mrs. Appelbaum began spending hours together after school and on weekends. They became friends and Mrs. Appelbaum began to teach Marissa jewelry making and repair. This unusual friendship surprised Claire, partly because before that time, which started shortly after Claire and Harry's separation, Marissa had been a pre-teen nightmare. She had been slamming doors, yelling, and intolerant of almost everything and everybody. Not fun to be around at all.

All of a sudden Marissa became a pleasant person. She was kinder to her little brother and tolerant of their neighbor, Tad, who used to irritate Marissa simply by breathing. Marissa used to think of Mrs. Appelbaum as an insane bag lady, but then she, as well as Roger, was spending many afternoons at Mrs. Appelbaum's home. They drank tea and juice, ate blintzes and bagels with cream cheese and nova and tomatoes at Mrs. Appelbaum's. They made jewelry. When Claire stopped by, she'd be pleased to see how comfortable her children were in Mrs. Appelbaum's home. Roger would be leaning back with the TV remote control in his hand. They began raving about Mrs. Appelbaum.

"Mama, did you know Mrs. Appelbaum and her husband used to have a jewelry store?" Marissa said. "He died a few years ago." Mama, have you ever seen those pictures Mrs. Appelbaum painted? Mama, have you seen how pretty Mrs. Appelbaum was when she was young on those old pictures? She's still a cute lady. I like to brush her hair when she takes down her bun. Her gray hair is so soft. When you look at her eyes real good, they're like brown marbles with little bits of gold. Mama, Mrs. Appelbaum survived the Holocaust. She's got these numbers on her arm that she said reminds her of really sad times. She's way tougher than she looks."

Mrs. Appelbaum was a dedicated follower of art history. She shared her knowledge with the Martin children. Marissa began passing on what she learned about the great artists and art masterpieces to Claire. Marissa favored Monet's paintings and had a framed poster of Monet's *Waterlily* painting in her bedroom. Claire was shocked beyond belief when she saw her tomboy daughter brushing Mrs. Appelbaum's soft, long, curly gray hair. In current days Mrs. Appelbaum would sometimes grab Marissa and hold her in a firm bear hug. "That windy day, young lady, you save an old woman's life."

Marissa once confided to Claire that around that time she was having silent conversations with Claire's deceased mother, Grace, and that this helped her see things and people differently. Claire accepted this as true because there had been times when Marissa seemed to be talking to herself. Claire could even pinpoint the timeframe she thought these conversations were occurring.

One Sunday morning, Marissa stood before Claire in a frilly pink dress that had hung in her closet for months. Claire had begged and attempted to bribe Marissa to at least try on the dress with no progress. Then that particular morning, a little princess dressed in pink appeared before Claire. Something was up. Photographic evidence of this monumental occasion was on a shelf in the den.

"Oh my goodness, look at you!" Claire had exclaimed. "Sorry to say it girl, but you look adorable. Absolutely adorable. Roger, come here and check out your sister all decked out! We're looking at a princess!

"Stop staring at me!" Marissa had growled in response.

Marissa had begun to outgrow her tomboy style in the past year or so, wearing less baggy shorts, oversized t-shirts and football jerseys, and more feminine tops and fitted jeans. However, that moment in the pink frilly dress and possibly three or four others would be the few times Claire would see her daughter in lace and frills.

When Marissa began wearing jewelry she and Mrs. Appelbaum had made, Claire became interested and jewelry making became a family affair. Soon they had accumulated enough pieces to start selling at school functions, flea markets and the senior center where Mrs. Appelbaum spent some of her time. Eventually they opened up the store. Sometime later Mrs. Appelbaum had fallen and seriously injured one of her hips. She considered moving into a nursing home, but Claire and Harry invited her to move in with them. It turned out to be a perfect fit.

Clothing was also sold at the Appelmar. There were new, as well as quality pieces that came from estate or yard sales. Some clothing was brought in and sold on consignment.

There was a seamstress on staff named Nora. She had a very short bleached blonde Afro. Her skin was a light reddish brown shade and there was a mole on her face near her mouth. She was a plus sized woman, about a size 18. She wore tasteful, but snug fitting clothing, lots of spandex pants with matching tops that came a little past her thighs, She liked big (often hoop) earrings.

Nora designed and sewed original items and also reconstructed vintage apparel. Nora had previously been a housekeeper who cleaned Mrs. Appelbaum's home several days a week. Clare was very impressed when she saw Nora out of her working clothes and in one of her own designs.

Nora was elated when Claire and Mrs. Appelbaum offered her the job as seamstress. They told her that she could receive a salary in addition to a percentage of each of her pieces that was sold. Claire knew that Nora had had a drug addiction in the past. Nora was one of nine children. Her mother, Lily, had pretty much raised the children on her own because the children's father, Roscoe, often disappeared on long alcoholic binges and to the homes of his other women. Claire had met him several times when he visited the store to borrow money from Nora. Roscoe was about five feet tall. He was almost light enough to pass for white and had full lips and a broad nose. When he tried to flirt with Claire she didn't say anything. She'd hold her left hand at his eye level, show him her wedding band, and continue what she was doing.

The job provided Nora with the financial security to escape an abusive relationship with her boyfriend Pookie. Claire had trouble believing that the extremely skinny man with the pimply brown skin, dreadlocks, and high cheekbones that made sharp points in his face could be responsible for the black eyes and bruises Nora attempted to hide behind sunglasses and makeup. The purple marks on her body could be seen from several feet away.

Nora had recently obtained her GED and was getting herself together. Claire hoped that Pookie would not lead Nora back into a destructive lifestyle. Nora called the relationship quits when she ended up in the hospital with a skull fracture and broken nose after one of Pookie's beatdowns. Pookie still made appearances outside the store.

For months, Juno, who was initially hired to help with heavy lifting and deliveries, was stationed at Appelmar's entrance. This was to prevent the scrawny Pookie from approaching the premises. Juno was a huge ex Sumo wrestler who was actually very kind and gentle, but his appearance was very intimidating. Pookie was no fool and stayed away from seeing distance of the store. He was eventually arrested for drug trafficking and sentenced to prison for a minimum of ten years. Claire hoped that the ten years was long enough for Nora to forget about the thug and find a nice man with whom she could settle down.

Nora was rising up in the fashion world. She had designed and made a spectacular beaded satin and lace wedding dress for a music superstar. Mrs. Appelbaum had designed the star's diamond earrings and necklace. Appelmar had made a substantial profit on both transactions. Other celebrities and even regular folk began frequenting the store and requesting one-of-a-kind pieces.

On this particular day, Claire was wearing a navy blue jersey knit pantsuit with flared sleeves and legs that Nora had made. The V-cut of the blouse was adorned with silver and black studs. Claire's earrings were silver drops with sapphire pear shaped stones. On her feet were black ballet slippers.

At Appelmar rolls of fabric lined a wall. Notebooks containing swatches as well as sewing patterns were stored on large bookshelves. Customers could walk in and choose from the store's selection or present some of their own ideas. The women at Appelmar had no doubt that their name would someday become a nationally known fashion line. They were beginning to research their options for having some designs mass-produced which would help them move into large retail stores.

When Claire and Mrs. Appelbaum entered the shop, Nora was at her sewing machine. Delilah, their other employee, with her dyed black spiky hair, black painted lips, black skinny jeans, and black top with the Rolling Stones tongue logo screen printed on it, was dressing a mannequin. Black hair was conservative for Delilah – she had been seen in pink or green hair. Her lips had been seen painted not only black but also purple or blue. She had piercings in her tongue, nose and belly button. There were three holes in each of her earlobes – three silver hoop earrings of different sizes in each ear. Her skin was like porcelain and along one arm she had a tattoo of some sort of vine with butterflies and purple flowers on it. She had very striking green eyes – Claire thought they were like some sort of luminous gemstone.

Claire met Delilah when Claire volunteered at a shelter where Delilah worked as an assistant counselor and where she had resided for a short time following her emancipation from foster care. She ended up in the system after her mother deserted the family. Her father had been unprepared to raise three girls. Claire and Delilah became close and when Delilah learned about the store, she hinted that she would like a job there. She said she was looking for a change.

When Claire visited Delilah's apartment the first time she was taken aback by Delilah's eerie skull collection; there were porcelain, plastic and wood skulls. Much of Delilah's clothing was adorned with skulls, but she had been discouraged from wearing those items to work because the skulls and skeletons rattled Mrs. Appelbaum.

Delilah also had a fascination for the *Wizard of Oz.* Alongside the skulls in her apartment were posters and figurines of Dorothy, the tin man, lion, scarecrow, Toto, the witches, the Wizard and munchkins. Every so often Delilah would show up in her Dorothy outfit – the whole get up - blue gingham checkered dress, white blouse, ribbon in her hair, white socks and a pair of red, shiny patent leather shoes on which Delilah had glued red sequins and rhinestones. For Delilah's birthday, Nora had surprised Delilah with the same style dress in several colors – orange, red, yellow and purple.

"Here," Nora had said. She handed Delilah a gift-wrapped box.

Inside the box were the dresses and a note that read: *Thanks for helping me pass my GED test. Some more Dorothy dresses.*

After opening the box and seeing the dresses Delilah ran weeping into the bathroom. When she came back out she grabbed and squeezed Nora. She said, "You didn't have to do that. That's one of the nicest things anybody's ever done for me. I love 'em. They're fab, awesome. Thanks, Nora."

"Yep," responded Nora, who never had a whole lot to say.

Delilah was in her mid twenties, a talented artist and a wiz at computers and technology. She was midway through a Bachelor's degree in Biology. At Appelmar she started out as a cashier but soon became involved in other aspects of the company. She designed an interactive website in which shoppers could post their photographs. Delilah would create an animated, proportioned version of the customer and the shopper could view images of herself or himself wearing downsized replicas of the clothing and jewelry. Almost like electronic paper dolls. Delilah was an illustrator and assisted Nora in creating some of the clothing patterns.

Delilah handled marketing for the store and was bold enough to visit movie sets and backstage areas of touring Broadway shows or concert arenas to drum up business. Nora's opportunity to create the music star's wedding dress had been organized by Delilah. Delilah had read that the singer had gotten engaged. The singer was shooting a video in Miami. Through a series of phone calls, Delilah tracked the singer down at a glitzy South Beach hotel and convinced her to let Appelmar handle her dress and jewelry.

Several hours a week Delilah volunteered at the women's shelter where she once resided. Claire was proud of all of them. The retail and online stores of Appelmar were quickly becoming huge successes. They were in the process of hiring cashiers. Television and radio commercials for the company had been recorded and were almost ready to be run. They had already begun to advertise in the small community newspapers with coupons offering 20% off of all purchases. Claire's hope was that they all could become financially successful through Appelmar.

Delilah's music choices (heavy metal and rock), with the loud screaming and screeching guitars, were shocking to Mrs. Appelbaum (as were some of Marissa's profanity filled rap music) but somehow they all got along.

"Okay, ladies," Claire announced. "Mrs. Appelbaum is here now and I'm out. Call me if you need anything." She hugged Mrs. Appelbaum before she walked out, whispering "everything's gonna be all right."

"Yes, yes, dahling," Mrs. Appelbaum answered. "Everything is going to be all right."

Then Mrs. Appelbaum addressed Delilah. "Delilah, what is that screeching you call music!" she yelled, "I have to cover my ears because of the pain it is causing me!"

"All right, all right," said Delilah. "I'll turn it down. Don't get so frazzled. Chill."

Nora was at the sewing machine, her iPod earphones plugged in, blocking out the sounds in the store.

Chapter 7

Harry rarely stayed in bed past 5 a.m. Even when he closed his office for holidays, it never occurred to him to be idle. He was always busy. He decided to take off work for the entire week. Fortunately, there were no scheduled trials and the cases he did have could be handled from his home. He had briefly spoken with his business partner, Dom, but did not give him specific details. He called Rosita and told her that he was giving her the week off with pay. She hesitated but was grateful for the opportunity to spend time with her new grandson.

This day while waiting for Claire, Harry decided to check out some television. He had heard the daytime names spoken around the house before: Judge Mathis, Maury, Judge Hatchett, Judge Judy, Jerry Springer, Regis and Kelly, Oprah and some others. He had never actually watched most of those shows. Harry was familiar with Regis but Regis had been around for decades. He knew who Oprah was. He would have to be living under a rock if he could not recognize one of the most successful, wealthiest women in the world. When he visited Appelmar during the day the televison would be on and often the women would be discussing what was on the screen.

Harry did not view much television in his present life. Included among the shows that he had watched during the past few years were *Six Feet Under, Seinfeld, Fraiser*, the WB's *Jack and Bobby* and HBO'S *The Wire* (which his daughter also watched). Some scenes in *The Wire* made Harry a little uncomfortable when watching with his daughter, but drugs, violence and profanity were part of the real world. He watched the *History* and *Discovery* channels. Harry tuned in to some televised sports and played video games with his son and daughter.

Harry picked up the remote control and Judge Mathis appeared on the TV screen. Harry had read about Judge Mathis and had attended several functions in which Judge Mathis was also present. He knew Judge Mathis was very involved in helping young men turn their lives around. But watching Judge Mathis on his show was something else. Harry noticed that if a judgmental plaintiff was not careful, he or she could find himself or herself on the wrong side of Judge Mathis' wrath when the plaintiff's own transgressions were revealed. Harry decided to add Judge Mathis to his TIVO schedule. This guy was a real character.

After Judge Mathis ended an audience began chanting, "Jerry, Jerry, Jerry" for the Jerry Springer show. Harry switched the channel and watched Regis and Kelly's talk chat. Regis and Kelly elicited a few chuckles from Harry. Then he turned off the TV.

Harry put on a pair of jeans and a polo shirt. Claire had started him on the track to being a more relaxed, modern dresser. In the past few years Marissa had given him suggestions on being a cool looking dad. He decided to cook breakfast for his wife. Standing over a pan making omelets, Harry started to think. He was prepared to have a difficult conversation with Claire. It was time.

Claire had no idea how she had rescued Harry from an empty, lonely life was the way Harry had seen it. There was never anyone else he felt that he just had to be with. Never. The thought of his cheating on her was as unimaginable as his ever walking on the moon. Before Claire, he had dated a few women, but it was basically something to pass the time. Over the years, during his time with Claire, there had been aggressive woman who had made romantic gestures toward him. After all, he was a handsome, successful man. There wasn't even a suggestion of reciprocation on Harry's part. Harry's total obliviousness to their seductions left these women frustrated. There was no need to confront him, or even avoid him because their actions, which included wearing short, tight, low cut dresses, and some nervy enough to go without underwear, went unnoticed by Harry. When they brushed up against him he would say, "excuse me" as if it were an accident on his part.

He was and had always been a loner. Claire was very popular, beautiful and graceful. What Claire's mother used to call his persistence was his need to be near this woman. After meeting her there were times when he would be so lovesick his stomach would feel so fluttery that he literally could not eat for days. He would force himself to put food in his mouth for sustenance, and then, only be able to nibble on small bits of food. Before becoming a lawyer and definitely before meeting Claire, he had never really fought for anything. Harry knew with a certainty that if didn't marry Claire he'd end up alone, a lifelong bachelor. If he ever voiced that aloud to anyone, they would question his confidence of that fact. He was 100% positive. He wept after they made love for the first time.

Claire sometimes said that she had been a selfish, inconsiderate bitch. In Harry's mind she was totally wrong about that. Some of the women she hung out with could be described that way but not Claire. Harry felt slimy thinking about it, but on occasions in the past, he had followed Claire. Stalked would more likely be the appropriate word.

The first time he saw her was in the late1980s. He privately called that moment his "lucky break." She was sitting on a blanket at the playground at a group home where Harry's mentor Mr. Gordon worked. Harry saw Claire for the very first time while he was gazing out of a window in Mr. Gordon's office.

Claire was reading to a group of kids. Her hair was cut in one of those stylish short hairdos, similar to Halle Berry or Toni Braxton's hair. Several little girls were trying to style her hair. They were making a mess but there wasn't a trace of irritation on Claire's beautiful face. When she stood up (wearing jeans, a red t-shirt and red and white sneakers) Harry noticed her glorious figure. She ran around the playground with the kids, swung on the swings, pushed kids on the swing, and slid down the sliding board. She was genuine and real when she smiled at the kids. *Oh, my God, she's got the most beautiful smile I've ever seen,* Harry had thought. Harry was truly enchanted.

On other occasions at the group home her arrival was like a movie star's visit. If they were outside playing all the children would run toward her. She would bring a huge bag with wrapped presents and snacks. Harry knew this because he followed her. Harry learned who she was from Mr. Gordon who was also once Harry's social worker. Mr. Gordon told him that Claire was a student at the same university Harry attended: the University of Miami.

Mr. Gordon allowed Harry to contact him even after he was no longer Harry's social worker. When Harry was in a miserable foster home, Mr. Gordon did everything he could to get him removed. Harry ran away several times from group and foster homes and begged Mr. Gordon to adopt him. Mr. Gordon explained that it was against the rules. He did, however, allow Harry to secretly spend some nights at his home. Harry was heartbroken when Mr. Gordon relocated to Florida to be near his aging mother. On the day of Harry's 18th birthday, which fell a few days after his graduation from high school, Harry caught a Greyhound bus to Miami and moved in with Mr. Gordon, his wife and their two young children. Harry didn't know where he would be if it wasn't for Mr. Gordon.

In spite of all of his difficulties, Harry managed to graduate with a 3.5 high school GPA. Mr. Gordon helped him complete his college and financial aide applications. Mr. Gordon was instrumental in getting Harry scholarships to the University of Miami, first as an undergraduate and then in the law school.

Discovering who Claire was on the inside made him love her more. Harry watched her deposit boxes of new school clothes on people's porches. Harry had actually seen her give someone her coat on a chilly day. If some homeless person begged for food or money, while her friends turned up their noses, Claire would slip the homeless man or woman money - bills.

"Why would you do that?" her friend Sharon would complain. "Once you give those people an opening they keep coming back for more." Claire would shrug her shoulders.

When her friends made fun of someone, only Harry noticed that Claire never laughed.

One morning Harry saw that Claire Connors had posted a sign-up sheet for volunteers to meet and discuss a food and clothing drive for a family whose house had burned down. Harry could not believe his good fortune. He bought a new outfit and got a haircut for a meeting that lasted less than a half hour. Claire noticed but didn't notice him. He hated parties but would go just to be near Claire. He wasn't affiliated with any organizations, but attended the Black Student Union, the school newspaper, the Student Democratic Party, and several other organizations' meetings because Claire was there.

Eventually Claire's eyes began meeting his eyes. She began acknowledging his presence and saying, "Hey, Harry." It became clear that if it were Claire who had called a meeting, Harry would be there to help her set up. If she needed help distributing flyers or anything at all, Harry volunteered. He rarely said a word, but thank God, instead of Claire becoming irritated or bothered, she accepted him with a polite graciousness. Deep down in his gut Harry knew that she was too kind to hurt his feelings. He knew she got tired of seeing his face. He knew she hated when he became friendly with her mother. Once, he drove all the way to Georgia because Claire mentioned that her mother had broken an ankle falling from a ladder, and he wanted to make sure she and her house were okay.

He would go to dances and parties with Claire when Craig was unavailable and Claire wanted a "safe date." Those events were way out of his comfort zone, but he went because Claire would be there and had asked him to go. He felt very uncomfortable on the dance floor, but he would dance when Claire held out her hand to him.

"Come on Harry. Let's do this," she'd say when the DJ played one of her favorite songs.

He had a basic side to side move and at some point Claire starting choosing his outfits. Because of these two things, people who did not know him probably assumed he was a cool dude with smooth dance steps and fancy rags. While Claire mingled he would find a spot in a corner and read. He always carried some book.

He was secretly thrilled that Craig never saw him as a threat. "Thanks for looking out for Claire," Craig would say.

"No, problem," Harry would answer.

He would be over the moon when he and Claire went shopping for outfits to wear to those Star Trek and Medieval events. He knew that she initially found them rather weird but she went along with it. Among those nerd-filled gatherings she stood out like a shining star. "Claire's here!" a Dr. Spock, Luke Skywalker or other costumed individual would inevitably announce shout at the functions.

He learned from Claire's mother that Claire had been a ballerina and pianist. Her mother would bring out awards, old photos and videos of Claire's performances. By that time Harry had already known he was love with Claire, but seeing her play the piano and dance gracefully across a dance floor helped to convince him even more that Claire Connors was the only woman for him.

Harry knew that Claire's friends found him very strange. Even as a little boy he had very little to say. This made finding permanent foster homes difficult. Some people found his silence unnerving. They would have preferred having a rambunctious hardheaded boy. People had difficulty discovering ways to punish a kid whose only insolent behavior was silence. Some of the people he resided with found their ways. They would try getting him to panic by locking him in dark places – Harry was used to that. They would try to get him to react by calling him derogatory names – Harry had been through that. They wanted to hit him, but that would mean losing the State money they received. As far as Claire, he didn't care what anyone else thought. He would hang around until she told him to stay away and that never did happen.

Harry knew that he wasn't as cool as some of the other guys, but he also knew that he was smart as anyone. He'd gotten modeling jobs so he knew he was pretty good looking. His looks only mattered to him if it helped him financially, or if it mattered to Claire. With everything Harry knew, none of it could prevent him from being a nuisance in Claire's life. He couldn't imagine living his life without Claire. He simply could not do it.

All these years later he still felt the same way. He remembered their first kiss and the first time they made love. Claire actually initiated both. He remembered how he would quietly enjoy watching Claire crying, singing and swooning during a Boyz II Men, George Michael/Wham or New Edition concert, or smile while Claire belted it out with Whitney Houston, Janet Jackson or Madonna. He would sit between Claire and her mother as they listened with misty eyes during a Johnny Mathis, Luther Vandross, Tony Bennett or Nancy Wilson concert. When Harry went shopping with Claire or with Claire and her mother, hewould bring a lightweight folding chair and books. Patiently and contentedly he would sit and read while the women shopped and tried on shoes and clothing at stores.

Harry thought about when he proposed to Claire, putting the ring underneath her ice cream while they were out to dinner. He was so nervous that she would choke on it. He thought about Claire's mother saying how much she enjoyed being involved in the wedding preparations and helping Claire to choose a bridal gown.

Harry thought about the excitement of their wedding day. There were over 200 people at the wedding. Less than 20 of those people were Harry's friends and family – Travis, Mr. Gordon and Mr. Gordon's family; Harry's friend and business, partner Dom; Dom's parents and two or three of Harry's acquaintances. Mr. Gordon and Dom shared best man duties. Claire had eight bridesmaids in peach dresses. The ushers who escorted the women down the aisle were Claire's family and friends. Harry felt not one ounce of jealousy over his future wife's popularity.

Their song for the first dance at the reception was "You and I" by O'bryan. Right after that they danced to "(I've Had) The Time Of My Life," (a song from *Dirty Dancing)* sung by Jennifer Warnes and Bill Medley. Harry had even lifted Claire up during that tune and didn't care one bit if he wasn't as smooth a dancer as Patrick Swayze.

Harry reminisced about their honeymoon in Jamaica, which was a gift from Mr. and Mrs. Dimaio. He and Claire relaxed on the beach and luxuriated under the sun.

He joyfully remembered the days his children were born and the first time he held them in his arms. On the day that Marissa was born he had been in court assisting Mr. Dimaio, his boss. He received a note to rush to the hospital. He was with Claire the whole time. He was in the delivery room when Marissa came into the world. Harry was in awe. When he held Marissa and looked down at her, already with those big, wise eyes, he thought *this beautiful little girl is mine. Thank you, God.*

They had been walking through Disney World during Marissa's first visit when Claire began having contractions during her pregnancy with Roger. When Harry laid eyes on the little boy in an Orlando, Florida hospital, his feeling of overwhelming joy was rejuvenated.

He remembered the days when he let go of their bicycles and they rode on their own for the first time. "Daddy, I did it! I did it!" Roger had yelled, his face beaming.

Harry had never owned a bicycle as a child. There were many things he'd never had as a child. He did everything in his power to ensure that his children would not know what that felt like. When he returned home after his and Claire's separation, they had a Christmas celebration during the summer: exchanging gifts, putting up lights and even eating a Christmas dinner.

Harry had a music cassette that he listened to repeatedly during his tormented love struck days. He purchased the cassette while strolling through a flea market. A label on the cassette read "Jonesin' for You Mix." Miraculously, Harry still had the cassette. Songs on the cassette included "Am I Dreaming" by Atlantic Starr, "Just My Imagination" by the Temptations, "I Wanna be Closer" by Switch, "I Do Love You," by GQ, "Be My Girl" by Michael Henderson, "Imagination by Earth Wind and Fire, and "Don't be Lonely" by Sho-nuff. Other songs on the cassette were "Seems Like I Met You" by Beau Williams, "Crazy 'Bout You" by Randy Brown, "Bullseye" by Lakeside, "Unchained Melody" by George Benson, "All I Do is Think of You" by the Jackson Five, "Love Jones" by Johnny Guitar Watson and "Come My Way" by Rene and Angela. There was also a song called "Dreams" by Smoke City, which was now playing in Harry's head. He had recently found a 45 single of "Dreams" after searching all over record stores and on the Internet. Most people had never heard of the song. *"I dream about you every night and day"* were part of the lyrics. Those words were quite appropriate to what Harry had and still felt about Claire. This day when he heard the key click in the front door, he had to hold himself back from rushing to grab and embrace her in his arms. Yeah, he was ready to talk.

Chapter 8

Even though their home was quite large, Claire was still able to smell the aroma of cooked bacon as soon as she opened the door. When they were dating, Harry would often cook for her. He used to make delicious omelets with tomatoes, mushrooms and herbs. He was a master griller of steaks, ribs, chicken, corn and anything that could be cooked on the grill. Her tongue was watering already.

The food was on their plates when Claire stepped in the dining room. Claire washed her hands at the kitchen sink. Harry was sitting waiting for her at the cherry wood table that could sit eight people. Claire sat down next to Harry.

"Okay, honey," Claire said. "Talk." She took a bite of the omelet and then ate some bacon. "Mmm. This is good. Whatever the problem is, we can handle it. Tell me."

"Sh-sh-she called me yesterday," Harry stammered. "Sh-sh-she called me."

"Who called you?"

"My mother, Myrlie. Said she's coming to town."

"Your mama's coming to town." *Finally, I'm going to meet her,* Claire thought. "I don't know why but I kind of thought she was dead," she said. "Why does this upset you so much, Harry?"

"We went through hell as children. Physical and verbal. She had this way of talking to you that hurt like someone punching you with their fists. I know they were just words but you never forget the sting they leave. She thought it was funny when one of us had to use the bathroom real bad while she kept the front door locked. She would deliberately do things to embarrass us in front of the whole neighborhood. All sorts of cruel mean things. She'd hang sheets outside if one of us wet the bed; the stain would still be there. Shout out loud that her useless boys had better learn how to hold their water. She'd call me tar baby when I'd be walking with other kids. Would tell me that she couldn't believe that something as black and ugly as she thought I was could come out of her body.

"She would come up behind us and thump us in the head by flicking her middle finger just because she felt like it. Beat us like a madwoman with anything she could get her hands on: belts, electric cords, shoes, books, wire hangers, tree branches, brushes that sometimes broke – anything. Sometimes she would chase us throughout the neighborhood if one of us ran. She said we deserved whatever beating we got whether we did anything wrong or not. The humiliation and degradation stay with you longer than the sting of the whippings. I've known men who got whipped nearly every day of their childhood lives and still ended up being criminals. I promised myself I would never hit my children that way.

"Sometimes she would go off for days and days leaving us with no food and neglecting to pay the light bill. Claire, it's hard for me to say this but I've eaten food that other people have thrown away. My brothers and I have gone through other people's trash to find things we can use. You think I'm creative when I invent recipes from canned and boxed foods. We had to learn how to do that in my home. I still thank God for the few neighbors whose houses we could go to for a home cooked meal.

"Claire, my mother is the kind of person who causes destruction everywhere she goes. Oh, Claire. I don't want to see her, but if I don't, she'll show up at my job. She'll ruin everything I have."

This was incredibly hard for Claire to comprehend. However, she'd spent time volunteering in homeless shelters and orphanages and knew that anything was possible. She knew that children were victims of unimaginable things. She even knew that abuse had long lasting effects, but she really never imagined that her husband had gone through such a troubled childhood.

"When is she coming?"

"She said she's supposed to be at the Greyhound station tomorrow morning at 10."

She grabbed his hand. "I'm going with you. We'll pick her up together. She can stay in a hotel if you don't want her staying here. Let's eat breakfast and spend the day together. And tomorrow we'll ride over to the Greyhound station to pick up your mother."

Chapter 9

Harry agreed to Claire's suggestion that they pick up Mrylie together. His nerves felt as if they were tied in tight painful bundles. In the eighties he dreamed that Mrs. Huxtable of *The Cosby Show* was his mother and Mr. Huxtable was his dad. He would come home with that look of frustration, and one or both of them would follow him to his room. They would talk and talk until he finally revealed his problem. Then they would hug and assure him that everything was going to be all right. At that time he wasn't a small child – he was a teenager, but he still had childhood fantasies. He had fantasized about being a member of the *Brady Bunch* with Mr. and Mrs. Brady as his adoptive parents.

Harry would fantasize himself as the sensible, laidback friend of Alex Keaton on *Family Ties.* He had seen reruns of *Leave it to Beaver* and as a boy imagined a mother like June Cleaver serving lunch to him and his obnoxious friend. He was still holding out hope that possibly Myrlie had changed.

Tuesday morning, Harry's children and Mrs. Appelbaum all watched him cautiously with worried looks on their faces during the breakfast he had prepared. Marissa's friend Kristin looked as if she felt sorry for him. When he dropped the girls off at school, Marissa kissed him on the cheek. Kristin said, "Thank you, Mr. Martin. I hope everything's okay." Ten-year-old Roger had pumped his fist, then patted his shoulder and said. "Don't worry, Daddy. Everything's gonna be all right."

When he escorted Mrs. Appelbaum to the senior center for her Tuesday morning classes, she held and patted his hand and face before he left. She hugged him tightly.

When he returned home he and Claire decided to take a stroll on the beach. It was still relatively early so the sun wasn't beaming down super hot rays. It was nice and breezy. Walking along the water's edge were egrets and other species of birds. Seagulls soared gracefully in the sky. Harry and Claire sat on a blanket amidst the salt filled air, mellow sun and calm water. Harry stretched out and placed his head in his wife's lap.

"I have two brothers and one sister," he said. "I should have told you about this a long time ago, but every time I thought about discussing it I changed my mind. Myrlie used to go off and stay away, sometimes for weeks. Sometimes when it was too cold we wouldn't go to school. Sometimes even if it wasn't cold we wouldn't go to school - I guess we just didn't feel like it. There wasn't anyone around to make us go.

"During one of our self-imposed school breaks we lost track of the days we'd missed. There were three boys and sometimes we did get a little rowdy: wrestling and jumping on the beds. Someone might have contacted the landlord. So, anyway, truant officers started coming around. They knocked and knocked. We tried our best to be quiet, but then one day there was banging on the door, and my little sister Lucy escaped before we had a chance to stop her. I suppose she was being nosy or maybe tired of being locked up. She might have been hungry. They forced us to leave. We fought, screamed and cried.

"Anyway, for a little while, we were together at the same location, but eventually we were all sent to different places. I've been through several foster homes. I haven't seen any of my siblings in a long long time. Through the years, I've thought about tracking them down but I never made a real effort.

From his wallet he pulled out a folded piece of photo paper and handed it to Claire. It was a 5 x 7 photograph that he kept in a hidden compartment in his wallet. The photo was yellowed and there were still creases when the photo was opened up.

"After they removed us from our apartment we were able to get a few things," Harry said. "I took this picture of me and my brothers and sister and was able to hold onto it for all these years. That's me," he pointed, "and that's my older brother, Billy. Lucy, the little girl right there and Lenny, the other boy, are twins. Billy, Lucy, Lenny and Harry. Those are our names. The names are not shortened versions of anything. It got a little old hearing teachers attempting to call us by our quote unquote proper names: William, Lucille, Leonard and Harold. We always thought the twins were bi-racial because of their light skin and curly hair. Billy was the only one whose father ever came around. Myrlie had a whole lot of boyfriends and a few husbands. When I spoke to her on the phone the other day, she said now she knew the identity of my father based on our resemblance.

"I used to picture someday being married and having children and a happy family, but I really didn't think I'd meet anyone special in real life. (He knew Claire hated when he made her out to be some sort of savior but he continued).

"When I saw you for the first time and then got to know how sweet and nice you were; when I met your mother and she treated me like I was some sort of grand prize you two had won, I couldn't believe how lucky I was. When your eyes started lighting up when I walked into the room, I used to pinch myself to make sure I wasn't dreaming.

"I had to hold back my tears when you and your mother surprised me with those amazing red velvet birthday cakes and presents you'd picked out especially for me. Slicing your mother's perfect handmade cakes almost broke my heart. They tasted amazing! With Dom's mother's cake and then your mother's cake, I'd have enough cake to last me for days and days. I loved the little birthday parties you and your mom would have for me. I would be over the moon when I opened those Christmas presents with my name on the tags. Helping you and your mom decorate Christmas trees and spending Christmas with you two was so exciting for me. You all have given me remote control cars, an electrical moving train with tracks, board games, a basketball and football. I felt like a kid in a candy store.

"And, when you walked down the aisle with your Uncle Louis in that satin dress (it was a fishtail, off the shoulder, v-neck ivory dress with hand sewn pearls and crystal beads sewn in flower shapes), I thought that you looked like a goddess! A beautiful mermaid. That dress was clinging to every single curve on your body. I could not wait to put my hands on you in that dress. You looked stunning!

"In the back of my mind I kept thinking that this has got to be some kind of dream. I'm going to wake up in the morning and discover that I was not really married to you. Me, Harry Martin, ending up with you - the woman of my dreams. I was on pins and needles until the preacher said, 'I now pronounce you husband and wife,' Do you remember how much I was shaking? I wasn't nervous about marrying you. I was terrified that you would change your mind.

"Baby, I know you despise it when I talk like this, but with you my life has turned out 10 million times better that I ever could have imagined. And that's not an exaggeration.

"I decided that I didn't want to take a chance on anyone or anything interfering with our lives. I love you so much; sometimes I still have to contain myself from running to meet you at the door every time you go out and come back. I'm scared that sometimes I'm going to hold you too tight. During our separation I thought I was going to die. I was so afraid that you were going to meet somebody else. Your mama passing away hurt all of so much. She was my family, too."

He inhaled deeply. "Since I heard from Myrlie, I've kind of been thinking about reconnecting with my brothers and sister. Maybe trying to find out what they're doing and where they are. But I'm scared about how it's going to affect our lives. And I'm nervous about what Myrlie's going to do to."

"Don't worry," Clare whispered. "No matter what, I'm not going anywhere. Don't you ever worry about me finding someone else. My mama didn't raise no fool. I love you too, Harry. Tomorrow we're going to the Greyhound station to pick up your mother. Then we'll take it from there."

Afterwards she leaned down and lightly kissed his lips. They had lunch together at a Cuban restaurant and spent the day checking out art galleries and museums.

That evening Mrs. Appelbaum cooked dinner. She'd called them earlier to say that her class had been canceled and that a friend would be transporting her home. She said that she had errands and would not be going to the store. Delilah and Nora had said that the store was relatively quiet and that they could manage. Mrs. Appelbaum informed Harry and Claire that she'd go on home and would be there when the children arrived home from school.

While Harry and Claire were out Mrs. Appelbaum had apparently gotten someone to take her to the supermarket. When Claire had Harry entered their home that afternoon they were met with an aroma of tantalizing cooked food. When they walked to the dining room Mrs. Appelbaum, Marissa and Roger were setting the table with a set of Mrs. Appelbaum's own china. The entire family sat down together to eat mouth-watering brisket with carrots, potatoes, celery and onions, and Mrs. Appelbaum's homemade latkes (potato pancakes). For desert Mrs. Appelbaum had cooked an apple pie.

During dinner Harry reminded the family about their upcoming volunteering commitments: helping serve food at a soup kitchen, assisting in the building of a Habitat for Humanity home, and helping out at an event in which disabled children competed against each other.

Roger complained about some girl named Rebecca who was all up in his face and aggravating him to no end. She was snatching and running off with his pencils. She was doodling on blank pieces of paper in his notebook. When he went to sit down in the cafeteria, she'd come from out of nowhere and steal the seat he had chosen.

"I know I'm not supposed to hit girls but she's starting to really make me mad." Roger said.

"♫Roger's got a girlfriend," Marisa sang.

"Shut up!" growled Roger in uncharacteristic anger.

"Stop it, Rissa," said Claire. "Roger, if she's really bothering you, I'll go talk to the principal," said Claire. "If she hits you, or if anyone hits you, you tell someone at school immediately and then tell me. Your father and I don't hit you and I'm not having anyone else do it, either. If someone hits you off of school grounds, and keeps on hitting you, I'm giving you permission right now to do what you have to do to defend yourself."

"If somebody hits you, you come to me," added Marissa. "I can dis you all I want to but nobody else better touch you. After I get through talkin' to those punks, I guarantee they won't be messin' with you again."

Roger nodded and then began animatedly talking about the big fifth grade end of the year field trip to Universal Studios.

"I can't wait for that trip. It's gonna be of the chain!"

The trip wasn't for months and until that day Harry knew they'd be hearing a lot of about it.

"Aww, Universal ain't 'bout nothing. That place is whack!" Marissa antagonizingly said.

"Shut up!" shouted Roger. "Universal's the bomb!"

"Whatever," mumbled Marissa.

Mrs. Appelbaum talked about the computer class she was taking at the senior center. "It is not as easy as it seem, using a computer, but everyone is going on the Internet now. I'm trying to get with the, how you say, program. Mariska, I would be happy if you could help me out sometime."

Hardcore Marissa had a soft spot for Mrs. Appelbaum.

"I'm go'n get you hooked up, Mrs. Appelbaum. Let me know when you're ready." Then Marissa casually said that Kristin would be coming home with her the following day and spending the night.

Even with the bickering between his children, Harry was touched to the very core of his heart, soul and stomach during dinner.

He had looked over at Claire who was rather subdued during the dinner. He knew that she was still worried about him. In a strange way he could hardly wait for the meeting with Myrlie to be done and over.

Later that night while Harry worked in the room he called his office, Marissa joined him with her schoolbooks in tow. Apparently Marissa was unable to sleep. She was dressed in a black t-shirt and long *Sponge Bob Square Pants* pajama pants. She sat in an extra chair situated in a corner but in Harry's view. "California Dreamin'" by guitarist Wes Montgomery was playing softly in the background. On the wall in the room there was a black and white picture of Sidney Poiter, as well as a picture of Gordon Parks, a picture of Tom Hanks and a picture of Whoopi Goldberg – a few of Harry's favorite celebrities.

People said Marissa was the splitting image of Harry, very dark brown (nearly black) smooth skin and large dark brown eyes, but of course, she did not wear her hair in Harry's low cut style. Harry's heart almost burst with pride as she sat there. He loved his children with every bit of his heart. When they got physically hurt in any kind of way, he would wish that he could take on the pain they felt. When he felt tormented by anything that happened in his past, he would immediately think about Claire, Marissa, Roger and Mrs. Appelbaum, and quickly reverse his thinking. If he had to pay the price for some of his past challenges to end up with this life, where he was rewarded with this family, everything he'd been through was worth it. He spoke to his daughter.

"Ree-ree, Princess, I know I've been acting kind of strangely for the last couple of days, but I'm going to explain it to you soon. Don't worry. I'm not moving out again. Your mother and I are doing fine. How about you and I taking a fishing trip in a few weeks? We haven't done that it in a while. We're going to start really putting those *Dolphin* and *Heat* season tickets to use. I can't believe how much you've grown. For Christmas, I was thinking we could all go to Disney World and Universal. I hope you didn't mean it when you said Universal was whack. I hope you haven't outgrown our trips to Orlando.

"Don't get embarrassed when I say this, but you know in my opinion, and mine is the only one that matters, you're absolutely the most beautiful girl in the world. Love you, Princess."

He rose from the chair in which he was sitting and kissed Marissa on the forehead, then returned to his chair and his work. Both of them sat there quietly; he working on some of his cases and Marissa doing her homework. Hours later, Harry Martin carried his fourteen-year-old daughter to her bed after she had fallen asleep in the chair.

Chapter 10

"That's her," Harry mumbled.

The sun shone so brightly through the windshield glass that Claire was led to shade her eyes with her hand. Upon first seeing Myrlie, Claire almost burst out laughing. Myrlie was a little tiny thing, less than five feet tall and no more than 110 pounds. Claire could easily take her out in one swoop. She still wasn't convinced that this woman could be the terror that Harry had described.

Myrlie was pretty with skin the color of butter. Her head was covered by a long blond curly wig or weave. Apparently, she had departed from a cold place because she was attired in a fur coat and black boots. It was at least 80 degrees in Miami. Myrlie pointed to her luggage with her eyes, hinting that she was waiting for Harry to get out and help her with her bags. Claire couldn't figure out how long Myrlie was planning to stick around because near Myrlie's feet were two large suitcases. Claire exited the car with Harry.

The moment Myrlie opened her mouth and started yapping, Claire could understand Harry's frustration.

""Damn, it's hot out here" were the first words out of Myrlie's mouth. "Harry, help me take off this coat. You sho' took yo' time gettin' here. I been waitin' fo' twenty or twenty five minutes."

Even though Claire knew that Myrlie's age had to be somewhere in the sixties, Claire still wondered why Myrlie couldn't remove her own coat. Judging from the first words spewed out of Myrlie's cherry-red painted mouth, Claire had decided that Myrlie was one feisty old lady.

Myrlie started up again minutes after sitting down in the back seat of the car. "You still black as night!" she said. "How you get this pretty woman? You still a boring ass nerd? What kinda boy like readin' books. That's all you used to do. Bringin' a flashlight in the bed wit you so you could keep readin' in the dark. Oh, my goodness. You was such a weird kid. Starin' at stars in the sky like they some big deal. This lady musta married you for yo' money."

Claire turned around in her seat and looked directly at Myrlie. Myrlie's dress was black with large yellow and red flowers. She wore large red flower earnings. She had false eyelashes glued to her real lashes and blue shadow on her eyelids. Close up her face revealed a little fleshiness, but overall she looked pretty good for a senior citizen.

"You got that wrong, Sistah," Claire answered. "I had him before he had money. How do you know he didn't marry me for my money? He could have every single penny I've got - he's so fine! I love my men tall, handsome and black as night. Harry fits all those qualifications, plus a whole lot more. And no, he's way beyond being a boring nerd. And if he was, there's nothing wrong with that. Bill Gates and those other billionaires are nerds. I'll keep Harry and let those other chicks keep those smooth, dumb ass dudes who are all stuck on themselves. This man right here is one of a kind and I thank God every single day that he's all mine. If you're here to trash Harry, you can go back to where you came from, Lady. It's not happening here."

"So, she do yo' talkin' fo' you. You still weak."

"No, he's not weak. He respects you because you're his mother, but you're not mine. My mother thought way too much of Harry to even think about talking him the way you are. She thought he was gorgeous and so do I. As a matter of fact, my mother was so crazy about Harry she probably thought he was too good for own daughter, because really, although it's not easy for me to admit this, he's a much better person than I am.

"Here's what we're going to do. We're dropping you off at the Marriott Hotel. We have a reservation for three days. You can hang out there if you want. I have two children and I'm not about to let them see you disrespect their father. Now you decide if you can behave yourself. If not, I can say I know what Harry's mama is like. She's a very pretty lady, but we didn't get to know each other very well."

They pulled up at the Marriott. "Here's the hotel and here's my cell phone number," Claire told Myrlie. "After we check you in I'm gonna have to ask you to not call my husband until you feel like you can treat him like a person. If I find out you've been causing problems for him at his job, it's go'n be on between me and you, lady. If I have to, I'll pick you up and carry you back to that Greyhound station myself. Harry, let's go check your mama into the hotel."

Chapter 11

Harry didn't know if he should be embarrassed or proud of the way Claire handled his mother. He should have stood up to her himself but he wasn't prepared. He felt like that same little boy who used to cry when Mrylie trashed him verbally or slapped him around. Through the years he'd learned to swallow his tears. Deep down, he wished that the meeting had gone down like it does on television sitcoms.

In his fantasy version, Myrlie would have said, "Harry, look how handsome you've turned out! You've done a fantastic job with your life! And who is this, your beautiful wife?" The three of them would have had a group hug.

The reality version was far less pleasant. Claire had become fed up when Myrlie continued to complain. Claire decided to find a seat in the lobby and wait for him there.

While standing at the reservation desk, Harry muttered to this mother: "The reservation's in my name." He didn't look at her. "I wasn't sure what your last name was."

"Prescott. Myrlie Prescott."

Harry instructed the reservation clerk to change the name. A bellboy came to help Myrlie with her bags. Harry took out two $100 bills and placed them in Myrlie's outstretched hand.

Myrlie looked at the money as if it was tainted. "How long this supposed to last me here in Miami?"

"Bye, Myrlie." Harry left her standing in the hotel lobby.

"Harry, I thought you were exaggerating when you told me about your mother," said Claire after they had returned to the car. Claire drove because Harry was still a little shaken up.

"She really is something else, a mess," Claire added. "Honestly, I felt like putting her across my knee and giving her a good spanking."

"She hasn't changed at all, except she's even smaller that I thought," responded Harry. "How do you think we can get rid of her without arousing suspicion?" Harry joked.

"That was a good one, Baby. She's a tough chick all right. I know you would never put your hands on a woman, but think about letting me get in the ring with her. She's a lightweight. I'm like a middleweight. I can and will take her down if you want me to.

"Let me think about that one. We'll see if her future behavior warrants a smack down."

"Say the word, Harry, and I will take care of her for you."

"By, the way, Baby," said Harry. "I couldn't help but keep on checking you out in that red top and blue jeans you're wearing. Those jeans look like they were painted on you. Other dudes were looking at you. You're still superfine! Man, am I lucky to have you!"

Claire smiled.

Harry was surprised and thrilled when Claire pulled into a Planetarium a short time later. Everyone close to him knew about his fascination for astronomy and stars. Harry and Claire sat for a while in a dark quiet room resembling a nighttime sky. Twinkling lights representing stars and the moon shone around them. They held hands. Harry laid his head on Claire's shoulder. He was beginning to feel better.

Chapter 12

Claire hadn't been this angry or so surprised in years. Just when she thought she had calmed down, she would find herself getting upset again. Myrlie had infuriated her, and Claire was shocked that she'd never seen the photo of Harry's family. All these years and she'd never once laid eyes on those people. She couldn't help but wonder if she really knew her husband. She couldn't help but think that maybe there was a flaw in her character that she'd never really pursued obtaining information about her husband's background? Was she that self-centered? These were things she'd have to figure out later on. Now she had to pick up Mrs. Appelbaum,

In her light green Jaguar, she swung into the parking lot of the plaza where their store was located, exited the car, and walked to the store entrance to collect Mrs. Appelbaum. This woman, Myrlie, was a piece of work. *Coming to town and putting down my husband,* Claire thought. Unbelievable.

Claire did not allow her children to disrespect adults, and she did not want to think about the confusion that would ensue if this woman were to begin a verbal assault on Marissa. Marissa had settled down and grown into a rather subdued teenager, but when someone crossed her path the wrong way, she could become hostile. For someone to mistreat her father, well, Marissa wasn't about to have any of that. Claire shook her head. When Harry said that his mother was coming to town, Claire could not imagine that spending a mere half hour with her could make her own temperature rise.

She worked in the store for a few hours and then the moment she and Mrs. Appelbaum entered her car after locking up, she released her pent up frustration on Mrs. Appelbaum.

"Well, Mrs. Appelbaum. I found out what's been upsetting Harry. His mother is in town. She called him a couple of days ago and now she's here. He hasn't seen nor heard from her in over twenty years and the first thing she does is insult him.

"Please, please, please, Mrs. Appelbaum. Don't say anything to Harry, but that mother of his is a flat out witch. You should've heard her putting him down. Mrs. Appelbaum, you know how wonderful Harry is. She talks to him like he's nothing, like he's nothing!

"I felt like crying! I don't condone physical violence but I felt like hitting her. I felt like picking up that little woman – my arms are thicker than her thighs - and taking her back to the bus station. I can't believe something in such a small package could wreak so much havoc. And get this, Mrs. Appelbaum. When we're waiting in the hotel lobby, she says, 'I know y'all ain't go'n leave me here with no money."

"I felt like taking Harry's hand and escorting him right out of that hotel! I left them and sat in the lobby before I started having a loud hissy fit in the Marriott hotel lobby. I left that situation in Harry's hands."

"Our poor Harry. His Mommy Dearest has risen again," said Mrs. Appelbaum, placing her hand on her chest.

"Boy, do you have that right, Mrs. Appelbaum! That little thing has the mouth of a truck driver. I told her if she couldn't behave herself, she wouldn't be allowed to step one of her tiny feet in our house. She looked at me like she wanted to kill me, but then she sat back in the seat and looked out the window. I couldn't see her eyes; they were probably rolling into the back of her head. I'm sure she was a little shocked. She's probably planning to retaliate against me. I could almost see the steam blowing out of her ears."

Dinner that evening was takeout: lasagna, spaghetti, salad and garlic rolls from one of the Martins' favorite restaurants, Antonio's. At the dinner table Roger announced that he was considering giving sports another try. He hadn't decided which sport yet but he'd let them know. In the past, Roger just did not like the grind of daily practice. That was something he and his chubby friend Tommy surely had in common. Marissa said that she was going to finish the softball season, and then try out for the girls' basketball team. The Martins did not push their children into doing anything they did not want to do.

Claire noticed Kristin sitting quietly at the table. She'd nearly forgotten that Kristin was staying another night. She wondered if it was her imagination but it seemed as if Kristin was slowly moving in. Kristin was wearing some of Marissa's clothes. The girls were good friends but had very different styles and personalities. Marissa preferred looser fitting jeans, high top sneakers and polo typed shirts, many with stripes or logos in the corner. Kristin dressed more girly with frilly and lacy tops, skirts, and feminine and dainty sandals. Kristin decorated her sneakers, bookbags and other things with sequins, glitter and *Looney Tunes Tweety bird*. Seeing Kristin in this black short-sleeved shirt with an orange *Nike* logo struck Claire's attention.

Kristin generally wore pastel type colors, pinks and purples. Claire would definitely have to have a conversation with the girls.

Harry was saying, "It's up to you, whatever you decide to do" regarding the children's sports plans. "By, the way, Rog Dog, I'm in the mood for taking you on in a li'l bit of *NCAA* on your Playstation after we finish up in here and after you've taken your bath. You up for it, dude? You're getting too big for me to keep on *letting* you win, so my game will be on, my brother."

"Dude, you never let me win anything. Maybe when I was two or three."

"We shall see," stated Harry.

Chapter 13

Harry and Roger did begin a basketball game on the Playstation III that night. Harry ended it when he realized they were going past Roger's bedtime and to the point where Roger had begun dozing off.

"Let's call this a draw," said Harry. "You're right. I'm not letting you win anything. You are tough competition. You don't mind if I walk with you to your bedroom, do you?" Roger nodded.

Harry lifted up the edge of a *Spiderman* comforter and Roger got into his bed, then under the comforter. Harry pulled up the chair from Roger's desk and sat next to the bed. Harry sang, "You are My Sunshine," a song he used to sing to the children when they were small. "You are my sunshine, my only sunshine. You make me happy when…" He stopped singing when Roger turned his face away from him. Roger's body began shaking. Harry heard him sniffling.

"Hey, Little Man, turn around. You're not crying, are you?"

Harry walked around to the other side of the bed with the chair in his hand. He sat next to Roger. Harry felt a stirring his heart when he saw his son's teary eyes. "I know you're sleepy but please sit up for a minute. I'll be right back."

When Harry returned to Roger's room, Roger, dressed in *Ben 10* pajamas, was sitting up with his legs across the side of the bed. Roger held his head face down. Harry gently held Roger's chin and raised Roger's head. Harry wiped Roger's nose with some tissue and wiped his face with a warm wet washcloth. He patted Roger's head. He looked Roger in the eyes and said, "You are a ray of sunshine in this family. Like that song says, 'You are my sunshine,' and that's the truth.

"Sometimes we probably put too much pressure on you because you are the one we count on to keep us smiling and laughing. If that becomes too much for you, remember that that is not your job. If you ever feel like breaking down and crying, don't you feel bad about that for one second. You can come to your mother or me anytime, with anything. If you're worried about me leaving home again; that's not what's happening. Again, it's not your job to worry about what's going on around in our home. For the record, I'm not going anywhere. That girl Rebecca thinks you're cute; that's why she's been harassing you. Get ready for some more of that because you're a real good-looking, talented, smart, charming guy, which is never going to change. But if she really starts to aggravate you, we'll have the teacher or the principal speak to her."

Harry kissed his son's cheek and forehead. "Love you, Rog. Love you a whole lot. Nod your head if you hear me." Roger nodded his head. Harry pushed the chair back a bit. "Now, stand up and give me a hug." Sleepy Roger stood up and he and his father hugged and Roger got back in the bed.

"Thanks, Man," said Harry. "Now I feel better. Tonight I'm going to sit right here until you fall asleep." Harry grabbed a few books from the book shelf in Roger's room. Although Roger might have been too old for the books Harry selected, Harry read them anyway. He read *Good Night Moon, Rainbow Fish* and *The Giving Tree.* Harry didn't leave Roger's room until he heard his son snoring.

Chapter 14

Harry's mentor and friend, Mr. Gordon, now owned and operated *U R Somebody,* a social services outreach center. There was counseling, after school tutoring, art and music lessons, and self-esteem and anger management classes. Harry and Mr. Gordon attempted to get together at least once a month for lunch. They were members of the same gym. Harry often volunteered to chaperone when the kids at the center went on field trips.

When Harry first met Mr. Gordon he was a husky twenty something former high school baseball player with a full fluffy Afro. He was now a fifty-something year old with a graying receding hairline. He was still in pretty good physical shape; there was a barely noticeable middle-aged paunch in his stomach. He had owl-like, dark-honey colored, welcoming eyes, and was a very attentive listener.

On Thursday, Harry stopped in to chat with Mr. Gordon. Mr. Gordon was chowing down on Popeye's chicken. John Coltrane's "My Favorite Things" played in the background. Mr. Gordon said he found jazz and classical music soothing – as did Harry. An appreciation for these music styles was something Harry picked up from Mr. Gordon so he quickly recognized Coltrane's smooth sax sounds.

Books filled several bookshelves in Mr. Gordon's office. Mr. Gordon's collection of horses of many shapes, sizes and materials including plastic, metal and wood lined the windowsill. There were horses on Mr. Gordon's desk and horses on the top of the bookshelves.

"Hey, playa, what's up?" Mr. Gordon greeted. He wore a red and blue shirt with *U R Somebody* embroidered on the top left. Mr. Gordon wiped grease from his lips. "Whew, this Popeye's chicken is so so good! Working it off is a mother but it's worth it. Check you out! Chillin' in the *Sean John* sweat suit and Nike's. Me likes."

Harry called him Chuck now. He blew out a gust of air and ran his hand over his close-cropped hair.

"Yeah, Chuck, Marissa bought this outfit for me. And my mother is in town." He picked up a horse and rubbed its back.

Mr. Gordon had seen him cry as a boy, but Harry did everything in his power to stop the tears from falling now.

"She called me Monday," Harry said, "and Claire and I picked her up from the Greyhound station yesterday. She hasn't changed. She embarrassed me in front of my wife; disrespecting me, putting me down. I hope she doesn't mess up the life I've been able to get for myself. She still has this way of making me feel like I'm a zero, nothing. In the last couple of days, I've started questioning and doubting everything I have and everything I am. I've been feeling like I'm this man who's pretending to be something that he's not. That maybe Myrlie's right when she tells me I'm this weird ass nerd."

"Listen up, Harry," Mr. Gordon said. "I've known you for going on thirty years now. I know you're a grown man and everything, but I'm gonna give you a pep talk like I did when you were a young git."

"I know you think you've been only on the receiving end of this friendship, don't you? You've never been aware of what you bring to the table. Even though I was limited in what I was able to do for you, you were always so grateful. Appreciation is rarely shown in this business. Your thank you letters were an inspiration when I considered going into a line of work. A kid taking the initiative to write a good word to someone is a special gift. No one taught you that. Your spirit led you into doing those kinds of things, and because of that I could feel like I was making a difference in someone's life.

"You probably don't remember a boy named Matt who was at the Finley House for a little while? Matt was a runaway who lived in one of those fancy neighborhoods. He and his father had had some kind of argument over a bad report card. It escalated and Matt ran away from home. Nothing I said cheered him up. I could not convince him to go back home. His parents were torn up and worried. You showed up one day and ended up sitting next to him. Even though you hardly ever spoke to strangers, you talked to Matt. You began tutoring him. Matt went back home. He told me it was something you said that encouraged him to go back. You told him you wished you had parents who worried about you.

"When my mother died," Chuck said, "and thank God we were given more years than we had expected, you sat with me for hours. I wasn't really up to long conversations with folks, but your quiet presence, my friend, was more comforting than a lot of the well-meaning words spoken to me by some others.

"My wife Harriett loves you. You would think that my own two children would be haters, with you moving in with us, and all that, but Benji and Emma think of you as their big brother. Harriett and I could go out knowing that you would protect and watch over our children. I know for a fact that Benji has come to you to discuss things he couldn't or didn't want to share with his old dad; things he knew would not be shared with anyone else.

"We social workers are not supposed to get attached to our charges. They say it's not good for business. But I'm glad I made an exception with you. You're my best friend. You've always remembered my birthday. I still have birthday cards from years ago that you've given me. And, Man, really, you have got to stop with those expensive presents. Some of the kids I deal with are hardcore and excellent thieves. That watch and some of that other expensive bling you've given me cannot be worn here at work.

"Every blue moon Harriet and I get dressed up and that's when I get to wear some of that fancy ass jewelry. You should see the diamonds on that Rolex glistening in the night. I was tempted to make you take it back, but hell, I figured you could afford it, big time attorney. And don't think I don't recognize the signature on those anonymous checks that arrive in my mailbox as contributions to this organization.

"Anyway, Harry, you're gonna get through this. People like your mom don't stick around too long, and even if she does, I'm sure you can handle her. You were always a good, strong guy. You've been through a lot but you made it. You have that fine wife and two great children. I was so happy when you and Claire got back together.

"Harry, you turned out to be a fine representation for the human race. I'm very honored to have you as a friend. I would give you a hug or a high five but my hands are very greasy. Love, ya, Man. Here, have a piece of chicken."

"No thanks," Harry replied. "If I never said it before, thanks for all the times you've stood by me. I'm not sure where I would be if it weren't for you. I really mean that. You were great during those hard months apart from my family. You've been like abig brother to me – a real brother. I really appreciate it all. Love you too, Man." Harry pumped his friend's fist.

Later that same day, Harry decided it was time to come clean to his law partner, Dominic Dimaio. He'd spoken to him by phone a few times with hasty excuses for his odd behavior, but had not revealed that his mother was in town.

Dom favored expensive silk shirts, fancy ties, designer suits (often in black), and thick gold jewelry. He liked expensive shoes. His salt and pepper hair was gelled and slicked back. Dom's father, Marco, was Harry's mentor in the law field. This was the first and only law firm in which Harry had ever worked. Harry had known the Diamaios since his sophomore year in college. While in law school, Harry as well as Dom had worked as all around assistants: paralegal, lunch retriever, courier, and sometime secretary. He and Dom were running the lucrative law firm now that the senior Dimaio had retired.

Dom's parents helped Harry obtain his first new car, cosigning for him and loaning him the money for his down payment. Dom's mother gave Harry birthday parties with full Italian dinners and baked him birthday cakes. He'd gone out to fancy dinners with them, been boating with them and eaten at their home many times. Harry was shy about letting the Dimaios know about his financial problems but Dom would inform them. They had been very generous about helping Harry financially. During his separation from Claire the Dimaios checked on him frequently.

Dom was about 5'8", still maintaining the fit, although wider, muscular build he'd had as a football player and wrestler during his high school and college years. His wife, Ramona, was at least 5'11' and towered over Dom in the 3-inch heels she usually wore. Ramona's nails were at least an inch and a half long and usually painted bright oranges and reds with elaborate designs. It was common knowledge that the two of them had met at the strip club where Ramona had been an exotic dancer.

When Harry entered his own office there were two stacks of unopened mail on his desk, apparently sorted by Dom's secretary, Felicia. One stack was a large stack of clearly junk mail. There was also a stack of telephone messages.

Felicia checked in on him. Her naturally curly glossy hair was cut in a neat, attractive short style. She was about the shade of a pecan shell and had slanted eyes like a Chinese person. Dressed in a black and white hounds tooth pencil skirt, white silk blouse, and black high heeled sling back shoes, Felicia said in her Jamaican accent, "You all right Mistah Mahtin? You want some coffee or anything?" He declined the coffee and told her he was fine.

After taking several hours to do catch up on work, Harry stepped into Dom's office. Dom was bobbing his head to Frank Sinatra singing "You Make Me Feel So Young." Harry sat in one of the leather chairs on the other side of Dom's desk. Dom looked up. Harry could smell the *Lagerfeld* cologne that Dom often used. Dom was wearing a burgundy button-down silk shirt. There was a white stripe around the collar and white stripes with swirly burgundy designs where the buttons and button holes lined up along the shirt. A little of Dom's black and white chest hair was exposed where two top buttons were undone.

"Harry, guy, what's going on? I know you mentioned that there's this problem you've been taking care of. Felicia's been taking your phone calls. I suppose you've seen the messages on your desk. You're not having problems in your marriage again, are you? We were very concerned about you back then. Everything fine at home?"

"Claire and I are fine, Dom, but my insane, ghetto fabulous mother, Myrlie, is in town. She called me here at the office on Monday and caught me completely off guard. I'm starting to get more comfortable with the situation. I hadn't seen nor heard from her in over twenty-something years. She sees my picture on the Internet. Says I look just like the guy she now knows is my father because of the resemblance, and before I can say anything, she tells me she'll be at the Greyhound station on Wednesday morning.

"So, Claire and I go to pick her up. Dom, she has not changed one bit. She's a short, petite woman, but Dom, my heart actually skipped a few beats when I looked into her eyes. The minute she gets into my car, she starts insulting me. She backed off when Claire confronted her. I was like a little boy – with Claire having to defend me against her. When I take her to the hotel, she had the nerve to say $200 was not enough spending money for her in Miami. I left her standing there with her hand held out. Anyway, Dom, I know it sounds crazy but that's the story. I'm all right. I'm dealing with it. Thanks for covering for me. I'm sorry for cutting out on you like that."

"Come on, Harry," Dom responded. "Why are you apologizing? So what, you need to take a few days off. We've been in this thing together for a long time now. Who would have thought after all these years that we'd still be not only partners in this law firm, but good friends as well? We randomly come together to do a sociology assignment during our sophomore year of undergrad and end up lifetime buddies. Ah, the things we've endured - interning for that slave driver boss - my dad. The chores he'd have us doing!

"You and I are going to become old men together. You never once judged me when I was going through the roughest stages of my alcoholism. Talk about covering for someone. I'd be so boozed on liquor I wouldn't realize that we'd won a case – some of my cases, in fact, for days after they were over. You've had my back 110%. There were times when you could have sold me out to my dad and didn't.

"I would have been totally screwed up if you hadn't shown up to handle that situation in Key West. Me getting blasted out of my mind. Then hooking up with some crazy chick who robbed me blind; stealing my wallet and my car. The only man I trusted with that was you Harry. You drove to the Keys to pick me up for goodness sake. You're like a brother to me. Do whatever you need to handle this.

"By the way, the old man and my moms have been asking about you. You know how wild my mom is about Harry. Hell, they still have your old blanket from when you spent the nights with us. My mother still sings that same old tune. 'Why can't you be more like Harry? Harry has never forgotten my birthday. Harry always shows up on time when he's taking me to an appointment.' Blah, blah, blah. And then Pops has made no secret of the fact that he's counting on you to keep this firm afloat.

"Anyhoo, the folks are having their 45th anniversary party in a couple of months and they want you and your entire family to be there. I know that you're not one for shaking your tail feathers on the dance floor, but Moms was hoping that Claire or Marissa could help her get a handle on the *Electric Slide*. They've started doing the Slide at the casino. All of us love you, Harry.

"Now, listen, Harry. Is there any chance that I could meet this firecracker mother of yours? Please, please, please. You've met lots of my crazy relatives. Can your mom be any worse that my Aunt Stella, with that obnoxious loud laugh, that fake suntan and those botoxed lips of hers? She swears she's Angelina Jolie's twin sister. Stuffing her plump, orange body into those tiny leopard print dresses.

"Or, how about my uncle Rico, with his shirts unbuttoned down to his navel, showing off his eighty-five year old wrinkly chest, and strutting around in his bell bottom polyester pants. He looks like freaking Don Knotts when he played the landlord Furley on *Three's Company*. Some of those outfits Uncle Rico has owned since the 70s. Every year at my family's Christmas party he shows up in his favorite white suit and red shirt and tries to imitate Tony Manero from *Saturday*

Night Fever. You've seen those performances so you know he's no John Travolta. Dad and I have had to warn him repeatedly to keep his bony hands and dry lips away from our secretaries? Really, Harry, I've got some loonies in my family and you've met most of them. Let me meet Myrlie. Let me meet your mom."

Harry was laughing so hard that tears were rolling down his eyes. His stomach was cramping.

"Stop it, Dom!" Harry cried. "This is supposed to be a serious conversation and you've got me laughing. Aunt Stella's my girl. And Rosita and Felicia have managed to get Uncle Rico under control. One time he did something to upset Felicia. Felicia was so mad she broke into her Jamaican patois. I'm not sure Uncle Rico understood what she was saying, but the fearful look in his eyes let me know he'd never bother Felicia again. Besides, he's getting too old to actually catch anyone.

"Take my word for this one, Dom. My mother is someone that you do not want anywhere near you. On second thought, how about if we trade mothers. Not only does Mrs. Dimaio love Harry Martin, Harry Martin thinks that Mrs. Dimaio is one special woman. Your mother and Claire's mother showed me what it's like to have real mothers. I'd never known what it was like to have someone bake me a birthday cake until your mother started having those little parties for me. I would be so choked up; I'd have to go the bathroom to compose myself. When Claire and I were separated, your mother cooked and froze so many meals that my freezer would be stocked to the rim with Tupperware containers filled with Italian food. How about this, Dom? Why don't we make up a legally binding document? I sign over my mother to you in exchange for yours. You don't even have to read the small print. I'm telling you up front that you'd be getting a really bad deal."

Dom silently pleaded with Harry through puppy dog eyes and pursed lips. Then he walked around the desk. Harry rose from his seat. The men hugged.

"I'll be back to work in full force on Monday," said Harry. "Thanks Dom, for everything. You and your family have been great to me."

"When can I meet you mother?"

"Bye, Dom."

Roy Johnson was Harry's neighbor. He was the father of Roger's best friend, Tommy, and worked from his house as a music features writer for a popular entertainment magazine. He'd had a couple of his books published. Anything someone wanted to know about music, Roy would know, or would be able to find. When Marissa had sports practice after school and was unable to be at home with Roger, the Johnsons' home was the place where Harry and Claire knew that their son would be well taken care of and loved. Although he and Roy had been acquaintances for years, they became good friends within the past year. Their older children, Tad and Marissa, were randomly paired together for a class science fair project, and this became the impetus that brought the two families even closer.

During his and Claire's separation Harry spoke to his children mostly by phone. Harry thought this would help to avoid overstepping Claire's authority and to give her the space she needed. He would still be in his children's lives. In the early stages of the science fair pairing, Marissa would complain constantly about Tad.

"Daddy, I can't believe what Mr. Switzer (her teacher) did! He's makin' me work on this science fair project with that old, goofy, aggravatin' boy, Tad. Call Mr. Switzer, Daddy. Tell him to put me with somebody else. Tad's gettin' on my nerves."

"It's not a big deal," he told her. "It'll be over before you know it." As a result of the collaboration Tad and Marissa had become friends. They did a project on the adaptation of butterflies to various environments and received a very good score.

After moving back home, Harry discovered that Tad, who had worn glasses for as long as he'd known him, was now wearing contact lenses. When Tad did wear glasses he sported fancier frames. The Johnsons were an interracial family. Roy was African American with medium brown skin and dark brown eyes. He was bald on top with hair on the sides and back of his head. Roy's wife Tori was a blond Canadian with aquamarine colored eyes tinted with greens and darker shades of blue. Their son Tommy's skin was like light caramel. His eyes were a light brown. Tad had a complexion similar to a cup of coffee with several spoonfuls of cream. He had green eyes with tints of brown. During Harry's absence Tad had become a hunk. He and Marissa sort of balanced each other out. Marissa had raised Tad's coolness level and through Tad, Marissa learned to accept kids who were somewhat unusual. In the long run, although Tad changed on the outside, he was a nerd and proud of it.

Even though Tad was what some called a nerd as Harry had also been labeled, Tad had something Harry did not have. Tad had nurturing, loving, proud parents who encouraged their unique son to accept who he was. Tad was a musician who played the saxophone, violin and keyboard. He was an athlete who excelled in basketball and a science and math wiz. He was a very nice, down to earth boy. And because he was so nice, he needed a tough chick like Marissa to keep the animals away. Harry thought it was a good friendship.

Tad's brother, Tommy (Roger's best friend), was a pudgy fellow. He had uncanny mechanically inclined skills. He was not very active, but when he put his mind to it, he could assemble a bicycle, repair eyeglasses and even some computers. He had a little toolbox. Harry liked the Johnsons very much.

When Harry drove into his driveway Thursday afternoon, he heard Roy calling his name.

"Yo, Harry!" Roy boomed. "Wait up a minute, Bro." Harry walked to the sidewalk to meet Roy, who was wearing a well-worn tight fitting Dan Marino *Miami Dolphin* jersey and green faded sweat pants from his alma mater, Florida Agriculture and Mechanical University. The FAMU logo, an orange rattlesnake (faded now), ran down one leg of the sweat pants. Roy was a hefty sized guy, with a moustache and beard. He wore glasses with black, rectangular frames.

"The boys are in the house," said Roy. "One minute they're arguing over some play and the next they're laughing all over each other. They were shooting hoops on our basketball court a little while ago. Laurel and Hardy. One skinny and one chubby. Two funny characters, sho 'nuff.

"But check this out," added Roy. "I've got four tickets to this gala where Barack Obama is the guest speaker. It'll be in January. Stevie's gonna be performing. Yeah, the legend, Stevie Wonder. I was wondering if you and Claire would like to join us. I believe Barack's got a chance of winning the presidential election. I really do! That speech he made at the 2004 Convention was phenomenal! There's the possibility that we might see a black man in the White House during our lifetime, Harry. I've been looking into volunteering for the campaign."

"I know," said Harry. "It's unbelievable! It's as if he just popped up from out of nowhere. The momentum's been crazy! I agree with you, Roy. He's got a chance. Claire and I would definitely like to be there. Claire's fascinated with Michelle Obama. Claire's going to be so excited."

"Oh, by the way," said Roy. "Tad wanted to know if you'd go with him to the *Star Trek* convention coming up. I offered to go but Tad says to me, 'Dad, you don't understand stuff like that.' He's right, you know. Science, *Star Trek*, science fiction – that kind of stuff goes over my head. Tori would go but she's got this work thing going on. Anyway, Tad wanted you. He's mentioned that you and he have had a few interesting conversations. He was really excited about a talk the two of you had about stars and astronomy that night we were all on the beach for the Fourth of July festivities. He says you listen to him when he talks. I'm not hating on that at all. We all need any kind of support we can get."

"Between me and you," said Harry. "I've been keeping tabs on that *Star Trek* convention, but if I even mention it to my children, it would be one more thing to make them hate me and think of me as the nerdiest father on the planet. I would love to hang out with Tad at the Trekkies *thang*."

"Okay, cool. Thanks. Stevie Wonder, Man! I've been dying for this. Every time he's come to town I've missed out on it. ♫ *Lookin' back on when I was a little nappy-headed boy,* Roy sang. "Let me go check on those boys," Roy said. "Boys can get a little rowdy. Talk with you later, Harry."

"Thanks for helping out with Roger, Roy. He feels so comfortable here; sometimes I think he believes this is where he lives. And everytime I think you've outdone yourself, you've put a bigger smile on Marissa's face. Introducing her to Jay-Z, Kanye, Justin Timberlake, Beyonce and all of those other stars. Getting backstage passes to concerts. Thanks a lot. For everything."

"No problem," said Roy. "I gotta start thinkin' about what I'm gonna wear to this big event with Barack and plus Stevie. My waist ain't what it used to be. I gotta be sharp. Hey, maybe you and I can hang out sometime."

"I'd like that Roy," said Harry.

This day when Harry entered his home, he immediately smelt his wife's amazing fried chicken. When he walked in the kitchen he saw a bowl of collard greens. In the refrigerator there was some potato salad and a pitcher of ice tea with lemon slices. There was a red velvet cake sitting in the middle of the dining table. Claire had stepped out on work early and had prepared a Sunday, but on a Wednesday, kind of meal. If things continued in this way, Harry's waist size would be on the increase. But he wasn't about to complain – not at all.

Chapter 15

Usually Claire transported Mrs. Appelbaum to her doctor's and other appointments but this Friday Harry was the designated driver. When he arrived at Appelmar Mrs. Appelbaum and her friend, Sadie, were cursing a person named Len who had apparently criticized someone.

"He is a mean mean man," Sadie was saying. "How dare he speak to him like that? I thought his performance was divine."

Harry assumed they were discussing someone they knew personally, but Claire explained that Len was a judge on *Dancing with the Stars,* and that Mrs. Appelbaum and Sadie were discussing a recent episode. Harry couldn't keep up with television personalities.

Mrs. Appelbaum was a reality show fiend. If she were watching alone in her bedroom, the family would hear her shouting at contestants or yelling at the judges. She loved *The Bachelor* and the Martins would be very aware of which girl she preferred or when she felt the bachelor made a dumb move. They would hear about it the next morning. She loved the *Real Housewives* shows on the Bravo network.

In addition to *Dancing with the Stars*, Mrs. Appelbaum also liked *So You Think You Can Dance.* She watched ballroom dancing on PBS. She loved biographical shows on artists, shows that focused on art history, almost anything that involved culture.

Mrs. Appelbaum, Marissa and Claire were regular viewers of *American Idol.* Mrs. Appelbaum shouted at Simon Cowell via the television screen when she believed he made especially harsh comments.

Through the years Harry had gravitated toward a few *Idol* contestants. From interviews he'd read and the radio, Harry became familiar with Ruben Studdard after Ruben's stint on *Idol* Harry became a fan of the hefty, mellow, former college football player and music major with the velvety, soulful voice.

One evening, Harry happened to be passing through the den when *Idol* was on and he saw Bo Bice singing "In a Dream." Bo's singing and the lyrics impressed Harry. Harry located a recording of that performance and saved the audio on a CD. He listened to it occasionally and had listened to it several times during the past few days.

Harry had returned Sadie to her condo and he was now sitting in the doctor's office waiting for Mrs. Appelbaum. While he waited he got caught up on celebrity gossip from *People* and *Us Weekly*. He was getting deep into an article about Brad and Angelina when Mrs. Appelbaum and Dr. Fisher entered the room.

"Well, Mr. Martin, here she is. For a woman your age, Mrs. Appelbaum, you are in good condition. Your blood pressure's fine, your cholesterol is good. I believe you've been eating well. I would even venture to say that you're well enough to go dancing. Just don't overdo it. Stay out of trouble, young lady."

"Pshaw," said Mrs. Appelbaum. "Oh, Dr. Fisher, you are too much. I will try."

Earlier, while driving to the store to retrieve Mrs. Appelbaum, Harry had passed a dance studio. He wasn't especially fond of dancing. Claire had to drag him onto the dance floor when they went to parties. He'd never become what one would call a party animal. However, something led him to return to the dance studio.

"Let's see what's going on in here, Mrs. Appelbaum," Harry said when they pulled in front of the studio.

Harry had anticipated that they'd meet up with a stern Russian woman whose hair would be up in a bun. He pictured the instructor as the type of woman he'd seen in movies; the type who strutted around the studio with very straight shoulders and pounded a ruler in her hand. Instead, Mrs. Appelbaum and Harry were greeted by a dark haired, pony tailed man, who introduced himself as Rodolfo. Rodolfo was about 5'6" with an extremely thin waist and virtually no hips. He was slim but appeared to be toned and healthy. He wore tight black pants and a purple satin shirt unbuttoned to the chest. He was bronze colored. Rodolfo checked himself out in the mirror that spanned the walls.

"Well, what have we here?" Rodolfo said, appraising Harry up and down. "We don't have the pleasure of seeing many chocolate hunks here, so indeed you are welcome." He turned to Mrs. Appelbaum. "Hello beautiful."

"My lovely friend has just received a clean bill of her health from her doctor," said Harry. "She loves ballroom dancing. I'm not crazy about dancing, myself. However, for my dear friend here, I'm willing to give this a go. What do you think, Mrs. Appelbaum? You feel like giving the ballroom thing a whirl? Think you can handle it?"

"Why, I would love to." cooed Mrs. Appelbaum.

"Come, come, come." Rodolfo grabbed their hands. "There is a tango class starting now. You can watch, and if you like, you can participate. No one expects you to be perfect. We are here to have fun."

Harry's spontaneous decision paid off. Mrs. Appelbaum thoroughly enjoyed herself. Harry was a clumsy dance partner for the women who took turns dancing with him. Still, they adored him.

"Promise me that you will return, Harry." Rodolfo pleaded and batted his eyelashes. "The ladies loved having you here. *And* I enjoyed having you here. You come back too, Elise," he said to Mrs. Appelbaum.

"Sure," answered Harry.

"I had a lovely, lovely time," Mrs. Appelbaum swooned from the passenger seat. "Thank you for doing this with me, Harry. We are all so very busy. We don't always have time to talk so much. I feel like I never get to thank you for everything you have done for me."

"Really, Mrs. Appelbaum, you don't have to do this. You're part of our family. You brighten all our lives. We love having you live with us. You have made a great impact on our children. There is no need for you to thank me."

"Yes, yes I do. I need to thank you. I did not know what I was going to do when I break my hip. In the hospital I cry at night worrying. I did not want to live in a nursing home and eat unseasoned food and stay in a cramped, cold room. I could have never asked to impose on you."

Mrs. Appelbaum began to weep. "For a month every day you came to help me remove years and years of clothing, furniture, everything from my house. After long days at work, on weekends, you help me clear out my home. In your home you never make me feel like I am a nuisance. I feel like I am part of a family. You cater to me when I could not move my body right after my surgery. I feel guilty because you never ask me for anything. My bedroom is lovely. You are my son, Harry Martin. I love you. Thank you. Rodolfo think you are a fine hunk of man, Harry. We will go back? Won't we? To dance?"

"Definitely. I love you too."

That Friday evening Harry decided to come clean about Myrlie to his family. When they were younger the children used to ask about their other grandma. He could not remember for the life of him what his responses had been. At some point the kids stopped asking. Since he hadn't been working during the past few days he'd been home every day to eat dinner with the family. This particular evening he thought that it would be nice to have a nice family dinner in a restaurant. Mrs. Appelbaum was at her friend Sadie's home. He'd already had the Myrlie discussion with her.

"We're all going out tonight for dinner," Harry had announced earlier to each of his family members: to Roger who was engaged in a football game on his Playstation III in the family room. Then Harry spoke to Marissa who was in her room listening to Kanye with her friend Kristin, and fiddling with a snow globe with the *Winnie the Pooh* characters inside. In Marissa's room there were at least 25 snow globes, about 15 from Disney World. Some snow globes represented various places the family had visited around the country. When Harry traveled on business he'd try to bring her a snow globe.

Lastly, Harry went to Claire who was in the kitchen perusing the refrigerator contemplating their options for supper.

"Okay," answered Roger, without missing a beat from his game.

"I was thinkin' about goin' to the movies with Kristin," responded Marissa. "Where we goin'?

"I was thinking about Luvey's. I'd really love it if we all went out together tonight."

"Ai-ight. Can Kristin come?"

Can't believe it was that easy, thought Harry.

"Sure, let her mom know she'll be coming home late."

"Can she stay here tonight?"

"Yes, call and verify that with her mother."

"Why not" agreed Claire when Harry told of her his suggestion for dinner. "I didn't take anything out of the freezer for dinner anyway. That'll be nice. I'm going to go change clothes."

Luvey's was a Caribbean/Soul Food restaurant in Liberty City. The walls were covered with autographed photos of celebrities who had dined there in the past. There was a small dance floor with a house band. Nino, the owner, had managed to keep the place family oriented.

Luvey's was known for gourmet and creative variations on Caribbean, Southern Soul Food and African dishes. There were various greens (collards, turnips) sautéed in garlic and red pepper, as well as chicken, fish and pork chops that were seasoned with exotic flavorings and served fried, baked or stewed. Conch and oxtails were also on the menu. Peanut butter, ginger, coconut and bananas were added to some dishes. The citrus flavors of lemon, orange or grapefruit juice were included in some foods and gave them a tropical zest.

"Yo ho, it's the Martins," jolly, portly Nino, the owner of Luvey's announced.

"Yep, it's us," answered Roger.

"Welcome, welcome. Someone will be here in a minute to take your order. Here comes Tasha now."

""Dang!" exclaimed Roger with wide eyes when Tasha approached the table. Tasha had a huge black Afro. She wore a net over it. There was dark purple glittery eye shadow on her eyelids and a bronze lipstick on her lips. She wore high platform shoes and a mini skirt that seemed be made with squared pieces of different fabrics, like a quilt.

"Look at Tasha's 'fro!" Roger shouted.

"Hey, y'all," Tasha said. "Roger, I dig your 'fro. What's it gonna be tonight, Martins?"

"Like yours too," Roger replied.

They ordered dinner and then a few minutes later Claire said, "Harry, the girls and I will be back in a few minutes. I need to ask them about something. Roger, sit here and keep your daddy company."

The subject of Myrlie never came up that night.

Chapter 16

They didn't hear from Myrlie until Saturday morning. Friday was the last night of her paid hotel stay. Claire received a phone call from an unfamiliar area code and telephone number. It was Myrlie's cell phone.

"Yeah, this Myrlie.," Myrlie announced over the phone. "Harry's mama. Some stuff came up and I gotta stay here a few mo' days. One a y'all gon have to change my hotel 'vation. Plus I'm go'n need some mo' money."

"This is Claire, Harry's wife," Claire said. "I'm not trying to get in your business, so I'm not going to ask you why you need to stay here. But for my family and husband's sake, I really don't think it's a good idea for you to stick around much longer. I've never seen Harry this upset.

"Now I know I can't tell you where you can or cannot go," Claire continued, "but I would like to do this. I would like to pick you up from the hotel, take you to the Greyhound station, and buy you a ticket home. I would like to give you $500 with a promise that you leave - tooday. That's what I'd want to do but you're Harry's mama. So, out of respect for him I'll let him know you called. If he decides he wants to do something different, I guess I'll have to go along with that.

"What I'm suppose to do 'til you get 'round to speakin' to Harry, and $500 ain't no money," Myrlie whined. "I'm go'n need mo money if you want me ta go back home."

It was all Claire could do to stop herself from screaming into the phone.

Claire took a deep breath. She felt like shouting but spoke tersely. "I'll extend the room for one more night. I'll discuss this with Harry. Even though I'd be relieved to see you leaving town, it's really not my place to make this decision. I'm telling you right now, if you say anything out of the way to my husband, you and I are gonna have a big big problem."

"I'm supposed to check outa here at 11. It's almost nine. I need you to hurry up and make my 'vation."

Claire slammed down the phone. She didn't have all day to deal with Myrlie. She had to get to the store, which was often quite busy on Saturdays. Mrs. Appelbaum usually went to temple on Saturdays, often spending Friday evening with her friend Sadie. Claire was in a hurry to get to the store. She decided not to disturb her children; letting them sleep in late. Harry had driven to the store. Claire quickly called the hotel and headed out the door. She'd call Harry later.

She was still disturbed about what she'd learned the night before at dinner. She noticed again that Kristin was wearing some of Marissa's clothing. In fact, it was one of Marissa's favorite *Old Navy* outfits – a red, white and black striped polo like shirt and black jeans. Kristin was wearing a pair of Marissa's red, white and black *Lady Air Jordan* sneakers. Kristin was a few inches shorter than Marissa and the jeans were rolled up at the bottom. The apparel was definitely not Kristin's style at all. The girls were almost dressed alike except there were green, yellow and white stripes on Marissa's shirt. Marissa was wearing wearing white jeans, and green and white high top sneakers. Claire had looked from one girl to the next. Both avoided her eyes. She told Harry that she needed to talk to the girls alone. Her instincts told her that this was an issue in which she should not procrastinate.

Claire had asked Nino if he had an office that she could borrow. He escorted Claire and the girls to a small room. In the room there was a desk with a computer, a calculator and papers scattered on it. There were three burgundy colored arm chairs close to the desk. Claire sat in the chair behind the desk and told the girls to sit down in the two chairs in front.

Claire leaned across the desk. She said, "What's up? Has Kristin moved in and I don't know about it? I've noticed she's been wearing your clothes lately.

"Rissa, you know that I don't care that she's wearing your clothes but I need to know what's going on." Kristin put up her hands and covered her face. She started crying.

"You know her daddy died from cancer a few years ago, right?" said Marissa. Claire nodded her head and placed a hand on top of Kristin's which were now folded on top of the desk. Kristin's head was bowed.

"But then her mama was sent over to Iraq for three years a few months ago with the army. She sent Kristin to live with some friends of hers. So the people's son has been tryin' to make Kristin do some nasty stuff. He's been fightin' her 'cause Kristin's been tellin' him no. Kristin didn't want to worry her mama."

Claire didn't want to think about what kind of stuff but she was able to whisper. "What do you mean, some sexual stuff?'

"Yeah, so Kristin ran away. She's been sleepin' at our house some nights and when she's not at our house, she's sleeping somewhere outside. "

"Okay," said Claire. "Let's go back to the table before the food gets cold. We'll talk some more about this later. We'll figure something out. Kristin, your mother needs to know about this. If she's called the house and not spoken to you, she's probably sick worrying about you."

When Claire got up from her chair she walked around the desk and grasped the weeping Kristin in her arms. She held the girl back a bit and moved several strands of yellow blonde spiral curls of hair from Kristin's face.

Claire looked into Kristin's tear filled sky blue (on a clear sunny day) colored eyes and said, "When people do these kinds of things, don't you ever think for one second that you've done something wrong. Don't feel guilty that you said something to give someone a reason to misinterpret your words. No one's got the right to put their hands on you if you don't allow them to. I'm talking to you too, Marissa. I'm proud of the way you're looking out for your friend, Rissa.

"Group hug," said Claire, and the three females held each tightly for a few minutes. "Kristin, we're going to go shopping to let you pick out some new clothes. All right, then, ladies. Let's get back out there before Roger comes looking for us."

When they returned to the table their food was there. Kristin was still sniffing. Everyone was silent. Even Roger seemed to sense that it was not a time for telling jokes.

Claire said, "If it's okay with everyone, Marissa and I would like Kristin to stay with us at our home for a little while. She looked Harry in the eye. "Harry, is it all right? I'll fill you in when we get home. Roger?"

"No, problem," said Harry.

"No problem for me either," added Roger. "Can we start eating 'cause I'm hungry?"

After dinner the family took a long relaxing drive along A1A and the beach. They eventually ended up at Jaxson's ice cream parlor in Dania where they shared a few delicious banana splits.

Chapter 17

In less than a week Harry had seen his life change dramatically. He was a man who (although he had moved around a lot as a child) liked the familiarity of a predictable life. The odd thing about Myrlie's unexpected visit and the resulting confusion was that once the initial shock was over, Harry had felt as if his heart was unbound and he was able to breathe freely. His normal schedule had been altered completely and he was enjoying the freedom of spontaneity.

He and Claire had decided to cover Myrlie's hotel stay for a week - a total of seven nights, Wednesday night to Tuesday night. Wanting to handle the matter with Mrylie directly and inform her of their plans, Harry decided to meet her for a few minutes at the Marriott Hotel's lounge on Saturday. Myrlie wanted to eat lunch so Harry agreed, thinking he would soon be rid of her. Myrlie ordered a t-bone steak, baked potato and a glass of champagne.

She wore a tight, bright orange stringy dress, similar to a twenties style flapper dress; and open toed, open backed high heeled orange shoes. The shoes criss-crossed across the top of her feet. On her ears were large orange star shaped earrings. On her lips was a shiny orange lipstick. At the restaurant Harry was turned off at her attempts to be classy – holding out her little finger and dabbing the corners of her lips with a napkin.

They sat in silence for most of the lunch. Harry didn't eat and sipped on a Coke for the duration. "Okay, here's the deal," Harry said. "You can stay until Wednesday morning. We're paying up to Tuesday night. That'll give you about an additional week. I'll give you a couple hundred dollars. After that, you're on your own."

"I'm go'n need money to get back home."

"We'll see about that. Now, I've got to get out of here because my daughter, your granddaughter, has a softball game at 3 o'clock."

"Harry, let me meet my grandchildren," Myrlie begged. "Please, take me to the game with y'all." Then she waved down the waiter. "Wrap these leftovers up for me, honey. I'm go'n take the bread too."

Against his better judgment, Harry said. "Okay, Myrlie, I'll let you meet them. But you say one derogatory thing to my kids and insult me in their presence and the meeting will be terminated instantly."

Harry dreaded allowing Myrlie to discover where he lived. He was becoming sick to his stomach weighing the options that were available to him. He thought about leaving Myrlie at the hotel, picking up his kids, then dropping Marissa, Roger and now Kristin, off at the field and going back to the hotel to get Myrlie. Another option was to pick up the kids and bring them back to the hotel with him to collect Myrlie. His mind was envisioning the future consequences of Myrlie having knowledge of the place where he found serenity and peace: his home. He was now at the hotel and the most logical, sensible plan of action was to take Myrlie with him.

Harry took a look at Myrlie's crazy orange outfit and decided he had to take a stand. Marissa would never forgive him if he showed up with a strange woman who would attract a lot of attention, not only from Marissa's teammates, but also anyone else who was attending the game. He knew what it felt like to have his mother appear at a school function in inappropriate clothing.

"Myrlie, that outfit is a bit much for a softball game," Harry said. "It's going to be kind of difficult for you to walk around in those shoes. I'll wait out here in the lobby for you to find something more comfortable to wear."

Harry was collecting brochures of South Florida attractions: Butterfly World, Metro Zoo, Lion Country Safari, South Florida Historical Museum, etc., when Myrlie appeared in the lobby nearly a half hour later. She was dressed in a knee length purple sundress splashed with pink, lavender and yellow flowers. A large straw hat was on her head. On her feet were opened toed shoes with sensible heels.

"All right, then," said Harry as they exited the hotel. "I mean it Myrlie. You are not allowed to degrade, insult or put down or my children or me in any way, shape or form. You are not permitted to say anything harsh to them. The minute you do this little reunion we're having will be history."

Myrlie had the sense to keep her mouth shut.

Chapter 18

Claire and her daughter Marissa were very different. Claire had a complexion similar to the color of a walnut shell with freckles and Marissa's skin was very dark brown, nearly ebony black. Marissa had big dark brown, almost black, dreamy eyes. Claire's eyes were hazel and almond shaped. Marissa's hair was usually in braids. Sometimes she wore it in ponytails and sometimes straightened and curled for special events. Claire's shoulder length brownish hair was straightened from chemical relaxers and most times she wore it parted on the side and curled under. For special occasions she might wear a French twist or other sophisticated hair style.

Monica, a woman Claire met at the shelter, permed and styled Claire's hair and braided Marissa's hair in their home. She said she enjoyed doing hair and cleaning. She cleaned the Martins' home three times a week while her four children were in school. The Martins paid her well and gave her a reduced rent in an apartment Harry purchased when he was single. They helped her buy a used, reliable car. Monica was starting to flourish and considering going to cosmetology school.

Mrs. Appelbaum said that Claire reminded her of a young Dihann Carroll. Claire and Marissa were both taller than average with long legs. Marissa was about 5'7" and appeared to be still growing.

As a girl, Claire enjoyed playing with and collecting Barbie dolls; Marissa had no interest in dolls. For years, a Barbie comforter that Claire had chosen covered Marissa's bed. A black and white zebra print comforter replaced Barbie about a year ago. Claire collected Disney movies, favoring those in which the regular girl ends up with the prince. She particularly liked *Beauty and the Beast* and became emotional each time she watched Belle and the Beast sing "Something There." She and Marissa enjoyed the *Friday* movies with Ice Cube, the *Austin Powers* movies and Tyler Perry's *Madea* movies. They knew lines from the movies after numerous viewings.

Claire relaxed by taking warm bubble baths, playing the piano, listening to music or reading. The Bible, *To Kill a Mockingbird, Wuthering Heights*, Toni Morrison's *Sula, and* Ann Fairbairn's *Five Smooth Stones (*which Claire's mother had recommended), were a few of her favorite books. She enjoyed works by Terry McMillan, Joy Fielding, Dennis Lehane, John Grishman, Walter Mosley (Easy Rawlins), and James Patterson (Alex Cross). She also liked books that reflected Florida's seedier side by authors Jeff Lindsay (*Dexter* series), Elmore Leonard and Carl Hiassen. She admired Jolayne Lucks, a lottery winner in Hiassen's book *Lucky You.* Her favorite poems were Maya Angelou's "Still I Rise" and "Phenomenal Woman." She could recite both poems by heart.

Performers Claire appreciated were Audra McDonald, Mary J. Blige, Sugarland, Annie Lennox, Alicia Keys, Janet Jackson, Latoya London, Jennifer Hudson and Faith Hill. Others were Andrea Bocelli, Maze, Joe Thomas, Rudy Currence, Angel Lopez, John Legend and Josh Groban. Gospel singers she liked were Yolanda Adams, Shirley Ceaser, Israel Houghton, Detrick Haddon and Donnie McClurkin.

Marissa was a fan of Sharon G. Flake's books. She had read each book in the *Gossip Girl, Twilight* and *Bluford High* series. She had an *American Girl* book collection on her bookshelf. Marissa previously owned many stuffed animals. The toy elephants, purple Barney, giraffes and other creatures had been relocated to a box in the garage.

Marissa listened to music on her iPod. She watched sports on TV and played video games. She participated in sports: basketball, softball and had run track in the past.

Marissa had a scrapbook with biographical information and pictures of athletes. Those included were Chad Johnson, Alonzo Mourning, Dwayne Wade, Jason Williams (*Miami Heat #55),* Derek Jeter, Ronnie Brown, Channing Crowder and The Rock. Other athletes in that book were Venus and Serena Williams, Tiger Woods, Michael Jordan, Alex Rodriguez, Peyton Manning, Donovan McNab and Lebron James. In another book Marissa kept information on entertainers: Bow Wow, Nick Jonas, Tristan Wilds, Dakota Fanning, Raven-Simone and Tupac. There was also Jesse McCartney, Usher, Lil Wayne, Lang Lang, the Beatles, Eminem, TLC, Chris Brown, the Jackson 5, Pink, Missy Elliot, and Beyonce and Destiny's Child.

Marissa was her daddy's girl. She had been her grandma's heart. Claire's mother, Grace, and Marissa had had a special friendship. Grace said that she (Grace) had been a tomboy as a child, as was Marissa. When the family visited Grace in Georgia, Claire would smile, seeing Grace, Harry and the kids climb trees to pick peaches and pecans. The female attorney who wore expensive suits to work would play kickball with her grandchildren in the grassy field near her house. Marissa and Grace used to bake pies and peach cobbler together. They would shell peas together. They shared many laughs.

Claire studied piano from age six up to tenth grade. She studied ballet from ages 5-15. An injured knee during a fall on her bicycle ended her dancing career when she was 15. She recuperated very well but lost the initiative to practice the hours required to dance professionally.

Marissa was also a writer/poet. She had a talent for putting eloquent words on paper. Her seventh grade Language Arts teacher, Ms. Sloan, had introduced her to the poems of Langston Hughes, Nicki Giovanni, Emily Dickinson and other poets. Ms. Sloan thought that Marissa had a promising future as a writer. She still kept in touch.

Marissa, however, was not flattered when Claire teared up and carried on when reading her poetry, essays or short stories. Or when her father copied them and carried them around in his briefcase. Claire ignored Marissa's rolling eyes when she boasted about Marissa's "genius for the written word." Marissa sucked her teeth and walked away when Claire asked her to read before grown ups.

"Okay, then, I'll do it," Claire would say. "Oh, my goodness," Claire would gush. "This is absolutely beautiful. My baby wrote this!

"Rissa!" Claire would yell. "I love this part. Come read it for us." Marissa would pretend she had not heard her.

Mrs. Appelbaum was no better. She would raise her fist in the air and shout, "Wonderful! Wonderful! That is our girl! Not only is she a wizard on the basketball court, she is a magician with a pen." Then she, Harry and Claire would give each other high fives and look adoringly at Marissa.

Marissa would mutter, "Those are some crazy old people."

Claire had entered college with a full academic scholarship. Like her daughter, she had been a smart girl. She completed her Bachelor's degree in Journalism in three years at Syracuse University. She took a semester off before entering law school and she and her mother traveled. They visited Europe: Paris, London and Rome. They took cruises to the Caribbean. They went to Hong Kong, Hawaii and various places throughout the United States. They shopped, took several cooking classes, ate exotic foods, and observed pigs being roasted. They visited museums and famous tourist attractions: the Louvre, the Eiffel Tower and Buckingham Palace. They went on an African Safari. They saw Niagara Falls, the Empire State Building, the Grand Canyon and other landmarks. When Claire looked at the pictures, she was extremely grateful for those moments spent with her mother.

Lately Claire had been searching for activities that would bring her and Marissa closer together. Maybe they'd take a trip together. It would be just the girls. Claire, Marissa, Mrs. Appelbaum, and if she was still living with them, Kristin, would all go somewhere together. The trip should be as soon as possible because Mrs. Appelbaum and Marissa were both getting older. In a few years Marissa would be going off to college and Mrs. Appelbaum... Claire couldn't bring herself to think about the consequences of Mrs. Appelbaum's aging.

Mrs. Appelbaum was still spunky; however, her movements were getting slower. Her fingers were curled over a bit and sometimes stiffened up. There were many wrinkles in Mrs. Appelbaum's face, which Claire thought gave her character. All of the Martins had really come to love Mrs. Appelbaum as a member of their family.

Saturday evening while Harry was out with Myrlie and the kids, Claire met up for an impromptu get together with her best female friends: Tori Johnson, her neighbor; Sharon, her college roommate; and Joy, a childhood friend. Claire was so grateful that all four women got along. She counted it as one of her life's blessings that her friends enjoyed one another's company.

Sharon had begun attending the University of Miami Law School by the time Claire returned from her months of travel adventures. Claire meandered through law school, taking a semester off here, dropping classes there. She met Harry in her second year of law school. He proposed during her fourth, but not last year.

Sharon had been the perfect size 5 during college. She was now a 12. She still had a lovely face and a voluptuous (enhanced by breast implants) figure. Her business attire included tailored, expensive clothes, mostly pantsuits and skirts with matching jackets. On her feet she often wore 3 to 5 inch high heeled shoes. Casual shoes for her were one inch high sandals. Once in a while she would wear blue jeans or shorts and sneakers, especially now that she was dating a younger man who was into outside activities. Sharon's long, reddish hair was highlighted with gold dye and made fuller and longer with extensions. Lately her hair had been cut in the feathered style of Farrah Fawcett's during the 1970s. Sharon said it was time for that hairstyle to make a comeback. She had brown eyes but wore emerald green or sapphire contact lenses.

Sharon had been dating her boyfriend Steve for three years. They met when he was part of a crew adding an addition to her house. Sharon complained that the younger, muscular, blonde, blue-eyed construction worker was not ambitious enough. Claire had a suspicion that Steve was not going anywhere. Claire had never seen Sharon so content in spite of her constant complaints.

In their college days Sharon could go overboard. Once, when they caught Craig cheating on Claire, Sharon spray-painted "Bitch" on his car. When her own boyfriends cheated on her, she would slash their car tires, break windows or make scenes, screaming and calling them derogatory names in public places. Claire had also been guilty of having a temper tantrum or two. They had been quietly asked to leave restaurants several times during their long friendship.

When Claire met Sharon's family, she was surprised to learn that bad ass Sharon came from blue blood Northeastern stock. Sharon's parents were the closest thing Claire had even seen to a real life Ward and June Cleaver. At that first meeting, it was obvious from Mr. and Mrs. Klausens' shocked - brief, but shocked eyes, that Sharon had failed to tell that them that her roommate, Claire Connors, was a black girl.

The shock was followed by several minutes of silence and then the Klausens questioned Claire about her home life and family. Back then, Claire was young and naïve and didn't give much thought to that moment. But as she got older, it hit her. She figured that most of the black people the Klausens had known were probably servants who had worked in their homes. The Klausens were rich and probably had black folks cleaning their houses and cooking for them since when they were children. Claire's own mother had put herself through law school by cleaning white people's homes.

Claire had never known if there was some sort of discussion with Sharon over her roommate's race. She didn't know if Sharon did not divulge the information due to fear, forgetfulness, or whether she was just interested in seeing how her parents would react. At any rate, over the years the Klausens accepted Claire into their hearts and lives.

The Klausens' home had been in the family for generations and to reach it, one had to follow a secluded winding road. When you visited Mr. and Mrs. Klausen's home there would be the aroma of homemade apple pies wafting in your nose. Surprisingly, it would be Mr. Klausen baking the pies from scratch. The Klausens grew herbs, fruit and vegetables in a garden, and rarely prepared anything from a jar. They would greet you at the door with wide, perky smiles and almost bone crushing hugs. Sharon's brothers, Lars and Chip, had that same enthusiasm. Both were tall, handsome, blond, blue-eyed guys who skied in the winter and surfed in the summer. When the boys lifted Sharon and Claire off the ground, the girls laughed and screamed. Chip became a scientist who specialized in research on epidemic diseases and Lars was an English teacher in an inner city neighborhood.

Claire found Sharon's parents charming but they annoyed Sharon. "Oh my, God," Sharon said one weekend shortly after they'd pulled into the Klausens' driveway. "Look at those freaks smiling and waving at us from the porch like lunatics. I hope they don't bring out the Scrabble game this time. I'm on a diet this week and they'd better not try to force feed me pot roast with all the fixings and all that sweet stuff they love to bake."

Claire and Sharon happened to visit the Klausens one Halloween evening. The Klausens were dressed as Raggedy Ann and Andy with floppy, red, mop like wigs and red paint on their cheeks. "So not cute," Sharon had said.

During the Christmas season the Klausens would have elaborate Christmas trees decorated with shiny, glittery, sequined homemade and store bought ornaments. Extravagant flashing lights would surround the exterior of the house. On the lawn there would be train tracks with running trains; a Santa with reindeer and elves that revolved around a plastic blow up globe; and a Nativity scene. Inside the home there would be a large homemade gingerbread house, homemade jams, jellies and all sorts of cookies. Underneath the tree the presents, including several for Claire, would be perfectly wrapped with swirly ribbons.

Even though Sharon and Claire were teenagers when they met, there would be stockings near the fireplace with the embroidered names of Sharon, her brothers, Claire, Sharon's brothers' friends, and even the pets the Klausens had at the time. Claire discovered that Mr. Klausen was actually the creator of many of the things in their home and the designated gift wrapper. Mrs. Klausen, who had degrees in anthropology and archaeology, was frequently busy in her job as an educational specialist at a museum. She wrote a large portion of the information given to students who visited the museum. Mr. Klausen had been a well-known hockey player and when he retired, he began a career as a home based interior decorator.

Mr. Klausen had been a big, burly man with bright red curly hair. Mrs. Klausen was a tall, big boned woman with blonde hair .When Claire did not visit the Klausens during the holidays Mr. Klausen would carefully pack her presents and Sharon would deliver them. Claire's goodies from her stocking would be packed neatly in a small box. Now that here parents were older, Sharon worried about them, especially her father, who was now partially incapacitated after having a stroke. He still maintained a jovial spirit. Claire saw them when they came to Florida for visits.

Sharon was currently a lawyer and felt that by now she and Claire could have been partners in their own firm. Sharon had been furious when Claire decided to marry Harry. Sharon said that Harry was the reason Claire had been so distracted, although she had been distracted before Harry. Sharon became a wonderful godmother to Claire's children, but she was not pleased when Claire became pregnant within a year of her marriage and dropped out of law school altogether. In their school days Sharon's vision of Harry was similar to Marissa's prior vision of Tad. Sharon used to think that Harry was the strangest person she'd ever met. Eventually, she conceded that Harry was exactly what Claire needed.

Although Sharon, as well as Claire, had been known to have tantrums, one thing for sure was that they had each other's backs. When Sharon's grandparents Klausen passed away in a car accident one summer, Sharon was devastated. She spent the summer with Claire and her mother. When Claire's father died Sharon made sure that Claire ate and maintained her coursework. Sharon visited Claire at the hospital during both of the children's births, bringing with her a carload of gifts. They supported each other during the difficult times of their romantic relationships. Through the years, Claire witnessed Sharon's soulful, gentle side when Sharon played quiet, melodious music on her guitar

During the Saturday get together Sharon revealed to the three women that she was beginning to feel insecure in her relationship with the twenty-something Steve. She told the women that she had recently purchased some sexy lingerie from *Victoria's Secret* and that she had "more than a few tricks" up her sleeve to keep her young man interested and satisfied.

Joy Robinson Levine was a math teacher who made a substantial additional income with a side job as a poet/songwriter. Joy wore her naturally auburn hair in twists. Her deep brown skin had reddish-orange undertones. She wore gauzy Indian peasant tops and skirts; long sleeved artsy seventies style buttoned shirts; sweat suits; and wide legged and regular jeans. Even though Joy could afford to shop at high-end stores, she enjoyed frequenting consignment and thrift stores.

Joy and Claire met in third grade when Claire intervened when several girls were teasing Joy at the private school they attended (Joy had been a scholarship student). They became good friends from that day forward. Joy and Claire lived 15 minutes away from each other. Claire lived in a more affluent neighborhood. The friendship began to grow when Joy started riding with Claire and her father after school. The first time Joy came home with Claire was when the girls worked on a school project together. Afterward, the girls worked on homework and class projects together in Mr. Connors' auto shop office. Sometimes Mr. Connors would close his shop early and he and the girls would go to movie matinees, get ice cream or tour local attractions.

Joy eventually began to spend many weekends at the Connors' home. She went on vacations with the Connors. She went shopping for school clothes with the Connors (Mrs. Connors bought a large portion of Joy's wardrobe). Joy was Claire's partner when the family went to drive in movies; the girls would run around in their pajamas. In all their years of knowing each other, Joy had never betrayed Claire's trust.

Joy's paternal grandparents and father, Ralph, raised Joy and her twin brother, Joshua. Their mother died when the twins were still babies due to a previously undiagnosed heart condition. While Joy and Joshua were growing up, Ralph had been an ongoing student in various fields as well as a freelance photographer. His income had been unsteady during the twins' childhood.. The financial stability in the Robinson home came from Joy's grandfather who worked for over 30 years as a sanitation worker. Some summers the kids traveled with Ralph while he photographed the world. Upon reaching 45 years old, Ralph became a serious student and completed his Bachelors, Masters and Ph.D. He became a psychologist in his fifties.

Joy's grandparents disproved the theory that if a person smoked cigarettes on a daily basis or overloads him or her self with greasy, fattening foods, he or she would die young. Joy's grandparents combined ham hocks and fatback with foods Claire would never think of as tasty food combinations. Their home smelled of seasoned, fried cooking oil, and cigarette smoke. For breakfast, which they ate almost every day, they would have greasy eggs, several types of meat – bacon and ham, ham and sausage, and pancakes or heavily-buttered grits. Claire had to acknowledge that although the food was heavy, it was delicious. She'd always loved eating at the Robinsons' home.

Mrs. Robinson was close to 300 pounds and Mr. Robinsons' weight neared 400 pounds and they weren't very tall. Claire would see them from time to time when they came down from Georgia to visit Joy. Claire was amazed that Joy had managed to stay slim with all of the fattening foods in her grandparents' home. Joy still wore size 7 clothing. At eighty something years old, neither of Joy's grandparents showed any sign of slowing down. Mr. Robinson still drove their car and they attended church every Sunday.

When Joy decided to marry David Levine, a Jewish black haired doctor with gray eyes, whom she'd met on an online dating service, the person whose reaction surprised her most was her father.

Joy said, "Claire, you know as well as I do that Tap (this is what she called her father) has dated many Caucasian women. He dated that French woman, Simone, for at least two years. He's dated Asian women, Hispanic women and black women. He says it's one thing to date a white woman but it's betrayal to marry a white man. I could not believe it when I heard him say that. Claire, my father is, or I thought he was an enlightened man. Not only does he have a Ph.D in psychology, he's traveled around the world photographing people of a multitude of races and cultures. He's slept in European hotels and straw huts in undeveloped countries. I truly thought he was better than that.

"I wasn't surprised at my grandmother's reaction," Joy said. "That woman complains when the sun is out and complains when it's not out. When I told her I was no longer eating pork, she acted as if I were insulting her personally. She says, 'So, I guess you too good now to be eatin' my cookin'. Next, you go'n be shame to say your granddaddy use to be a garbage man.' That garbage man's job provided my brother and me with a stable home and put me through college. There's no way I would be ashamed.

"She says she always believed that I wished I were white the way I used to carry on about those 'new boys on the street,' referring to New Kids on the Block. She forgets or doesn't want to remember that we were crazy about New Edition, too. Says she's not surprised I would choose to marry a white man. 'All the things white folks put us through. Now you go marry one of them,' she says. I think to myself that David has been nothing but nice to her but I don't say anything. I let her talk until she's run out of things to say."

When Joy told Claire about that conversation, especially the part about New Kids on the Block, Claire would've bet every penny she had in the bank that Mrs. Robinson brought her (Claire's) name into the mix. Not only did Claire have a light complexion, she had studied ballet and piano. Her mother had been an attorney. Since elementary school Claire and Joy had been like two peas in a pod and did almost everything together. Claire could still remember the irritated way Mrs. Robinson glared at them when they broke out in silly teenage giggles.

"I wish I didn't have nothin' to worry 'bout. I wish I had the time to laugh over foolishness," Mrs. Robinson would say. When Claire would arrive to pick up Joy in the red Mustang she received from her parents as a graduation gift, Mrs. Robinson would look at the car with her lips pressed tightly together. She would complain, "Lord, why your parents bought you that car. Now I got one mo' thing to worry about. Joy gettin' hurt. I could sho' find mo' important things to do with my money. What's wrong with the two of y'all takin' the bus?"

Joy was too nice to repeat the portion of Mrs. Robinson's rant that included Claire. Ever since they were children Joy had a mature kind of common sense. She had been a fantastic friend to Claire.

"I love my grandparents so much," Joy said. "I've called my grandmother sometimes three or four times a day and I suppose when she sees my number on the caller ID she won't pick up the phone. I can't believe she's written me off like this. When I'm speaking to my grandfather, he'll beg her to talk to me. Even though she can be fussy, she never failed to show my brother and me how much she loved us. I'm determined to break her down. I want my children to get to know her and my granddad.

Joy said, "Before I even got pregnant, David's mother asked me to promise that I would not give her grandchildren names ending with "wanna" or "nequa.". "Once she presented me with a Tina Turner sort of wig and asked that I wear it when I visited her home. She said that it was difficult explaining to her friends what the "locks" or "twists, whatever" were all about. She said I would be more attractive if I stopped dressing like a hippie. When David told her I was pregnant, she must have said some horrible things because they got into a big argument. They haven't spoken since. She never came to the hospital to see the twins and has not met them. One of David's sisters has never looked me in the eye, but his other sister, Laura, who just turned 25, has been great. She offers to baby sit and we go shopping together.

"My grandfather, Joshua, Laura and David's dad have visited our home to see the twins, but we're not allowed to mention their visits to anyone else in our families."

Saturday night Joy said that she'd invited everyone in her family and David's family to her twins' second birthday party.

"Neither my grandmother nor Mrs. Levine has seen the twins in person," said Joy. "I've sent them pictures. We'll see what happens.

"I hope my house will still be standing when I arrive home this evening," Joy added. "The last time I left Ariel and Ariana home alone with David, they emptied out my cosmetics bag. Liquid foundation and lipstick were mashed into my bedroom carpet. Lipstick drawings were all over the place. He wasn't able to get all of the makeup off of their faces. They'd gotten to one of my notebooks containing poetry and song lyrics and added their own touch. I'm not sure how my housekeeper, Betty, removed all the lipstick from the mirrors and furniture. The carpet was ruined. From the destruction you would've thought a group of boys had trashed my house and not two little girls."

Joy picked up her Bottega Venetta purse (a birthday present from David) and pulled out her cell phone. "Excuse me. I'm going to call home, just to make sure those two tiny hellions have not harmed my husband." Before she got up, Joy took a sip of her Shirley Temple.

Tori Johnson came to the United States from Canada after finishing college. She was several years older than the other women. She had silky, thick blond (with natural streaks of silver) hair that hung down her back. People stared at her striking eyes trying to decide the actual color. When she and Claire were out together, people would ask them where they'd purchased their contact lenses. Tori exercised diligently and it showed in her toned body. She looked great even in the blue jeans, khaki pants, polo shirts and button down shirts she wore to work. Her work as a construction engineer required her to be in the sun often, so her face and arms had a natural golden glow, which was enhanced by an inner contented spirit. She and Joy were *Claymates*

(Clay Aiken fans) and *Fanilows* (Barry Manilow fans). Tori had been a fan of Donny Osmond from girlhood to the present.

Claire and Tori became friends through their children. Their sons Roger and Tommy were always at each other's houses. When Claire's mother was sick and living with them, Tori would come sit and talk with her when the Martins had gone out. Claire and Tori became even closer during the infamous school science fair project the year before. It was unbelievable now to think that that at one time Marissa thought that Tad was the most annoying thing since Steve Urkel.

Claire could tell when the boys spent their time with Tori because Roger would come home with handmade masks, papier-mache animals or paper or Lego structures. Tori was very patient and she'd do all sorts of craft projects with the boys.

Tori's parents divorced when she was thirteen years old. Her father had been a car salesman. The story that Tori told was one day her father sold a yellow Camaro with black lighting strikes to a tall, super thin brunette librarian named Hannah. A few days later he made a pit stop to Tori's family's home and loaded up his clothes in the Camaro. He moved in with the woman. He had a second family with the woman. He didn't live very far so Tori, her mother and siblings would run into him every now and then. He provided very sporadic financial assistance.

At the time Tori's mother was a housewife. To support her three children she took a job as a waitress in a hotel lounge. In the evenings Tori would often help her mother clean. The owner overheard Tori singing along with the jukebox one night and hired her to perform in his club. From there, Tori became a well-known performer in her community. Not only was she able to help her mother financially through singing, Tori was also able to pay her college tuition and expenses. Claire was impressed when she learned that as a teenager Tori had made several music albums.

Tori had told Claire how she met Roy. She had gone out to a sports bar with some of her friends. She heard several guys talking and laughing. "One of them had the heartiest, happiest, most infectious laugh I'd ever heard," Tori said. "I got up and it was as if there was some sort of string or rope pulling me along. It was as if someone had grabbed my hand and was guiding me past tables and chairs through the bar. I found myself standing near this table with five or six black guys who were having friendly debates about sports and politics.

"Then someone told a joke and Roy broke out into that laugh. I looked at him and was enchanted by that gap between his teeth and that twinkle in his eyes. The dimples in his cheeks were what topped it off. His baseball cap was turned backwards on his head and his mouth and lips were greasy from chicken wings they were eating. From that moment on, it was like that Carole King song. I felt the Earth move under my feet.

"Roy was definitely not what I would call my type," Tori had said. "First of all, I'd never dated a black man before, and secondly, the guys I did date were very health conscious and reserved, I guess more like me. Roy was a little on the pudgy side even then. Claire, you've met some of Roy's friends. They're gorgeous even at our age. Back then, they were in their prime. So, it wasn't even as if Roy was the best-looking guy in the place. I can't tell you what it was.

"Even though I've always loved romantic movies, *An Affair to Remember, Love Story,* I'd never really believed in love at first sight, but here it was. I felt as if my heart would explode out of my chest.

"One of the guys nudged Roy because I was just staring at him. When Roy looked at me I turned around and rushed back to my table. All night long, even though I managed to stay connected with my friends, I kept a watchful eye on Roy. I've never been the kind of woman who chased after men. My friends were following my eyes, but were too confused to question why I was staring at that other table.

"Then Roy walked over to our table. 'Do I know you?' he asked me. I could not speak. He said 'Do you want to talk to me about something?' I was subconsciously aware of my friends averting their eyes and playing with the ice in their glasses or twisting their napkins.

"Finally, I was able to say, 'Yes, I'd like to talk to you.' I walked ahead of him and managed to find a semi-quiet corner in the bar.

"'I'm not sure what this is,' I told Roy. 'I've never done anything like this,' I said. 'But there's something about you. I know it's crazy but I think I'm in love with you.' Roy said, 'Excuse me?' He looked around him as if he thought there were other people in the background somewhere. Later on he said he thought he might've been on one of those TV practical joke shows. He has also said he'd never been involved with a white woman.

"I gave Roy one of my business cards with my home telephone number written on the back and quickly walked away. About three weeks later he said he was going through his wallet and found a business card with my name and number."

When Roy told the story of their relationship, he says Tori was too humble to repeat his exact words during that first phone call. Roy said he told her, "Oh, you're the sexy, blond chick with the most beautiful blue eyes I've ever seen in my life. The one who looked real good in those blue jeans from the front and the back. You're the one who was playing around with me at the bar."

Tori related that she told him not only did she mean every word she said, but also that she had returned to the bar several times looking for him. "I convinced him to meet me for lunch," Tori said. "We talked for hours, really not realizing how much time had passed. We went to an art festival in the park, walked around and listened to musicians that were playing there. We spent that whole day together and it felt so natural. We decided to wait at least a month before we slept together, although there was a lot of making out. He made me laugh so much and the rest, as they say, is history. That was nearly twenty years ago and so now I am a real believer that love at first sight does exist. He encourages me. When I'm feeling insecure, he builds me up. He's wonderful."

"Yes, he is," agreed Claire.

"My mom did have one comment," Toni said. "She said that if I was going to marry a black man, why couldn't I pick someone charismatic like Sidney Poitier. I told her, 'Mom, Sidney Poitier is old enough to be my father.' One of my brothers stopped speaking to me and one of Roy's sisters rolls her eyes at me and says as little as possible. She'll say 'excuse me' if she has to gets past me or small things like 'pass the salt and pepper.' Roy's mother, as you know, Claire, is incredibly sweet.

"'Come give Grandma some sugar,' she says to my boys and all of her grandchildren.' Her pink or red lipstick is all over their faces because she doesn't settle for one kiss.

"Sometimes Roy and I get stares on the street. Sometimes his talkativeness and high energy wears me out a little, but his personality was the thing that drew me to him in that bar. Approaching him that night was the truly the best decision I've made in my entire life. I wouldn't give up my family for anything."

On Saturday night, Tori revealed to the women that Roy had been encouraging her to try to revive her music career. He wanted to do an updated version of the album she had made in her teens. He also thought that it would be a good idea to add in several new songs. He thought it would be cool to have some rappers do a few lines in a few of the songs.

"Joy, do you have any songs that I could use?" Tori asked.

"Sure. That would be great!" Joy responded. She had returned to the table and said that somehow David had gotten the twins to go to sleep. "I love your singing! I'll go through my stuff. I know for sure I've got something for you."

"And Claire and Sharon," said Tori, "what do you say about brushing up on your piano and guitar? We have a keyboard at the house. We could put together a little band of women on the verge of middle age."

Sharon said, "We'll call ourselves the Sisteristas." They all agreed that Sisteristas would be a good name.

Since Claire had vented to the women individually about Myrlie, she did not bring her up again. She drank her Martini and enjoyed the company of her friends. The Sisteristas had decided they would have their first practice session the next week. Claire hadn't really played piano in a few years, but she had been tinkling with Mrs. Appelbaum's piano. Her fingers, body and soul were tingling with the anticipation of seriously getting back into playing real music on the piano's ivory and black keys in actual performances.

She was beginning to feel rejuvenated. Before opening up their store, there were moments when Claire had begun to feel unfulfilled, especially now that her children were growing up. Being a stay at home mom no longer kept her as busy as it used to. The flexibility of owning her business allowed her to be there for her children and renewed her sense of accomplishment. She was thinking about completing her law degree. Now, she and her friends were planning to start a band. She was excited thinking about what the future might hold for her and her family.

Their lives were slowly returning to normal, although Claire knew that things would never be quite the same. In a sense she felt that might not be such a bad thing. Harry was feeling better and returning to work on Monday and the children were doing well in school. She was pleased about the the health report from Mrs. Appelbaum's doctor. Appelmar was doing steady business. Nora and Delilah had devised a great idea for coordinated ensembles. They had gotten a fantastic deal on a batch of exotic silk, satin and other quality fabrics in various shades and designs from a liquidation sale. Customers were given options to mix and match outfits with skirts, pants and jackets. Kristin was getting comfortable in her new home. Myrlie was still in Miami, quiet, but still in Miami.

Sunday morning while she and Marissa cleaned the kitchen before going to church, Claire and her daughter had a conversation. The family had had a lovely breakfast with Harry's *Super Duper Strawberry Topped French Toast*. Harry had also cooked bacon, home fries and eggs. He made a freshly squeezed orange, grapefruit and pineapple drink with cherries.

Marissa said, "Mama, I believe she did Daddy wrong."

"Who did your daddy wrong?" asked Claire.

"His Mama. That lady, Mrylie. I don't feel like callin' her Grandma."

"You don't have to. Call her anything you want but don't get vulgar. I'm proud of you for your looking out for Kristin. I need you to trust me with stuff like that. We're going to definitely check into what can be done about having Kristin live here with us. If anybody ever tries to touch you in an inappropriate way, you come to your father or me immediately. I know we've talked about sex before, but I want to remind you that whenever you get ready to become intimate with boys, come to me. I promise I won't judge you. I want to help you make the best decisions now so that your life is not messed up down the road.

"I can't believe how beautiful you are. Harry and I sure did produce some gorgeous children. I love you, Rissa. I was thinking that you, Mrs. Appelbaum, maybe Kristin and I could take a little trip together. Roger and Daddy can do something together."

"I'm okay with that," said Marissa. "I love you too, Mama."

"Give Mama a hug and kiss," said Claire.

Chapter 19

While Harry believed in God, he wasn't a man who attended church every Sunday. If there was any moment in his life when he felt like his faith was being tested and that he could use a spiritual connection, he thought that time was now. The week had started out horribly with Myrlie's Monday morning phone call, but amazingly, Myrlie's visit had resulted in a positive turn of events in Harry's life. Harry began connecting with his friends and family in ways that he had never done before. The burden of withholding his unhappy childhood from Claire had been lifted. Harry decided he would attend church with his family.

Reverend Jones had baptized both of the Martin children. Even though Harry wasn't a frequent visitor to the church, it wasn't due to the charismatic pastor's sermons. Reverend Jones was over seven feet tall. He was a black man with light skin, naturally curly hair and blue eyes. Women flocked to the church in hopes for more than spiritual fulfillment, but Reverend Jones was all about preaching the Word. It was common knowledge that the reverend had passed up a lucrative opportunity as a chemical engineer with a major company to pursue the ministry. Before that, he had accepted a full academic scholarship in lieu of a full basketball scholarship to a top ten college.

He had pursued a graduate degree in chemical engineering and then worked as an intern with a major corporation that cleaned up water sources and built homes in a poverty-stricken African country. The images he witnessed struck him so deeply he decided his life's calling was serving God and people. He spent several years in Africa after the internship ended, working with nonprofit organizations.

Harry found Reverend Jones lively, funny, sincere, open minded, and thought that he delivered intelligent, insightful messages. Harry always found him intriguing. Reverend Jones had counseled Harry and Claire during the difficult time of their marriage.

The choir and congregation had just finished singing "Amazing Grace" when Reverend Jones walked up to deliver his sermon. Sitting between his wife and son, Harry listened intently as the reverend began to speak.

"I am the Master of My Ship. I am the Captain of My Soul," Reverend Jones said. He read the entire poem.

"That poem was written by William Ernest Henley in the 1800's," Reverend Jones added. "When I first read that poem I did some research on the author and learned that as a young boy he suffered from tuberculosis and had a leg amputated. He had many health problems during his lifetime but he continued to persevere. This poem reminds us of the power we have to make the most of our lives and difficult situations. The poem emphasizes how much we are strengthened when we let go of blame and that "why me" attitude. I'm here to state that with God, anything is possible. With God, any obstacle can be overcome, including the hurdles of anger, blame, unforgiveness and loneliness. We can accomplish so much when we believe in ourselves and in God.

"Many of you have probably heard the story about Joseph, his coat of many colors and his brothers. In the story from Genesis 37:1-36, Joseph's brothers betrayed him. They tried to destroy him. Joseph was the son of Jacob and Rachel. He was sort of like a miracle child – his mother Rachel was unable to have children for a long time and Joseph was born to Jacob when Jacob was an old man. Joseph tried to do the right thing at all times. Joseph was his father's favorite son. His father had given Joseph a coat of many colors.

"Joseph had several dreams. One dream was that he and his brothers would tend binding sheaves and this his brothers' sheaves would bow to his. He dreamed he would lead over his brothers. A second dream of Joseph's was that the sun, moon, and 11 stars bowed to him.

"One day, Joseph reported to his father that some of his brothers did not work as they should. The brothers, jealous and angry, sought vengeance against Joseph.

"Jacob, Joseph's father, sent Joseph out to find out how his sons were doing tending flocks in Shechem. When Joseph set out to find his brothers, he learned that they had left Schechem and went to a place called Dothan. The brothers saw Joseph before he noticed them. They kidnapped him, threw him in a pit, and left him there. Other brothers of Joseph discovered him in the pit and sold Joseph to Ishmaelites for twenty pieces of silver. When Joseph's brother, Reuben, and some of the other brothers returned to the pit, they discovered that Joseph was no longer there, but his coat remained. The brothers took Joseph's coat, tore it, and dipped it in goat's blood. They told their father that Joseph had been killed. They used the tattered coat as proof that Joseph had perished. Joseph's father was devastated and mourned for many days.

"Joseph was sold by the Ishmaelines to a pharoah in Egypt. Through his hard work, he eventually became an overseer. There was a famine and Joseph's brothers were some of the people who had suffered. They had to come back to him for favors, which included grain for food during a famine. When they first approached Joseph, they did not recognize him, but Joseph knew who they were.

"Joseph was able to forgive his borthers. He helped them find work. He provided them with grain for food. Joseph believed and told his brothers that it was not them, but God, who was responsible for him becoming a slave. God was responsible for the trials and tribulations that he went through. God helped him ultimately become a successful man, and in a position to cultivate grain that provided food for people to survive. The bottom line is that Joseph forgave his brothers.

"Each of you can probably think of someone who's done you wrong and you're having trouble forgiving him or her. Think about everything Jesus and Joseph went through. Jesus was arrested, beaten and mocked. When he informed his tormentors that he was king of the Jews, they dressed him in a purple robe and a crown of thorns to taunt him. They rolled dice to determine who would receive his clothes. They nailed him to a stake between two criminals. He was mocked while he was on that cross.

"Jesus forgave the men who crucified him. In Luke 23:34, Jesus pleaded with God: 'Father, forgive them, for they do now know what they are doing' Joseph forgave the brothers who tried to destroy him.

"Forgiveness does not mean you have to become best friends with the person who's wronged you. You do not have to invite and embrace them in your life. You will probably never forget the act that was perpetrated against you. But you can forgive.

"Forgiveness means letting go of the anger and hurt that makes you feel that your guts are tied in tights knot. It means releasing the anger and hurt that grips your mind and takes up space in your thoughts where positive, happier thoughts should be. It means throwing out that anger and hurt that dwells in your heart that prevents you from loving with all your potential. Unforgiveness could prevent you from living the richest, fullest life possible to you. I know forgiveness is not easy.

"I'll be the first one to say that I've held some grudges in my life. Holding onto grudges felt like a heavy load of sand I was carrying around with me. When I've been able to let them go, I tell you I felt like a freed man. Free yourself. Forgive - today.

"And loneliness. We don't always think of loneliness as a burden but it is. The world is a harder place when we try to make it alone. There are far too many people on this planet for someone to feel totally abandoned. Sometimes we, ourselves, have to make the effort to connect with others, to connect with God.

"Our communities have changed, our world has changed. With the improvements in technology, it is possible for us to live in a world of virtual isolation. There are times when we can be content with our gadgets and ourselves. However, there's nothing like a connection with other people. There's nothing like a connection with God. And since there is a God, we're never really alone. God is always with us.

"Some of you sitting in this church are dealing with some heavy things and feel like there's no one you can share your troubles with. Talk about it with God. If you believe you're not sure how to go about it, come to me and we'll pray about it together. Talk with the people who love you. Talk to the stars, talk to the waters on the beach, talk to the sun, to the moon. Talk it out. Release your burdens Remember, God never ever gets tired of listening.

"On the flip side, we can and should make ourselves available to our neighbors and others whose burdens might be heavier than our own. That is part of our obligation as Christians – to look out for others who are less fortunate that us. Check in on your elderly neighbor and bring him or her something to eat. Help out the single mother raising her children alone. Help out the brother who's making a real effort to bring himself up after being incarcerated or strung out on drugs. Let's all help each other get through our struggles. We can't and shouldn't have to do it alone. Amen.

After church on Sunday, Harry picked up Mrs. Appelbaum, brought her home and then he went grocery shopping. In the car he listened to "In a Dream." "*In the morning when I wake. And I'm blessed by God's grace. Just to open my eyes and see your face*" he sang with Bo. The weather had been holding up pretty well for the past few days and so far this day was sunny and warm. Harry was in the mood to barbecue by the pool in their back yard. He had changed into a pair of cargo shorts and a T-shirt.

After returning home from the store Harry put on the apron he wore when he barbecued. Red lettering that read "World's Greatest Dad" was printed on the apron. The apron was a Father's Day gift from Roger. Harry put charcoal in the grill and even though it was October, he blasted his summertime music compilation disc on a large boom box. The CD included songs such as Fresh Prince and DJ Jazzy Jeff's "Summertime," Sly and the Family's Stone"Hot Fun in the Summertime," Chicago's "Saturday in the Park," War's "Summer," the Beach Boys' "Surfin USA," Faith Hill's "Sunshine and Summertime,"and other music.

Harry had purchased ground beef for burgers, steaks, ribs, chicken and corn on the cob. He persuaded Claire to prepare potato salad, string beans and a pound cake.

As he cooked food on the grill, Harry thought about Reverend Johnson's words and reflected on the subject of forgiveness. He was certainly struggling with many emotions including how he would choose to deal with Myrlie.

Saturday afternoon when he and had Myrlie arrived at his home, he got out of the car and then went around to open the door on Myrlie's side. Opening car doors for women was a habit, something that he did unconsciously.

When he walked toward his front door, Harry ignored Myrlie appraising his house with wide opened eyes. The Martins' home was located in an older neighborhood with many trees and manicured lawns. The houses were large and original in design. The properties were well spaced apart with spacious front and back yards. Children rode bicycles; roller-skated, glided on skateboards, threw footballs, jumped rope and played in the street. Sometimes the adults played cards in the yards and people talked across their fences.

In the Martins' own back yard, there was a swimming pool and a covered patio with table and chairs. In front of the house there was a basketball goal.

Harry and Claire had made several investments that increased their weatlh. They had purchased several stocks that turned out well. The law firm had won a few multi-million dollar class action suits. Appelmar was successful. Harry's old apartment building brought in additional income. Claire's mother left them some money (she had set up college funds for both children).

Still, Harry's clients had constructed most renovations to the Martins' home, including the large open kitchen with its island and granite countertop; the remodeled expanded bathrooms; and two additional bedrooms. Although he worked primarily in corporate law, Harry had gotten many poor men out of tough legal and criminal situations. In exchange for financial compensation to the law firm, the men through their varied talents had gratefully helped to create a home that looked like a famous person's mansion. Harry would also feel compelled to give the men money for their time and efforts.

When he opened the door, Harry allowed Myrlie to enter first. Harry took in the decorative marble tile in the front room. Mrs. Appelbaum's burgundy and tan paisley printed furniture with its carved wood arms added sophistication and class to the room. An Oriental carpet was in the middle of the floor. There were several African busts and masks. Large original paintings by Jonathan Green (a man and woman dancing by the sea) and artist Charley Harper (birds luxuriating at the ocean side) graced the wall. An elaborate crystal chandelier hung from the ceiling in the living room. Mrs. Appelbaum's piano glistened from a corner in the room. Some of Mrs. Appelbaum paintings were up in the living room. Harry's favorite painting by Mrs. Appelbaum was an image of a green grassy field filled with red, yellow, and orange tulips. Two redbirds, their beaks pointed toward a bright yellow sun, flew just above the flowers. A pale blue sky with wispy clouds filled the background. .

Harry was no longer interested in impressing Myrlie with his possessions and accomplishments. The only thing that concerned him at that point was that Myrlie not inflict his children with her hurtful tongue.

When he and Myrlie entered the family room, where there was cushiony brown leather furniture (two reclining chairs and a long couch), an arcade sized air hockey table, bookshelves filled with books, and a custom made entertainment center with stereo equipment and a 40-inch plasma flat screen TV, Roger was engrossed in his Playstation. Bart and Homer from the *Simpsons* animated cartoon were zig zagging across the screen in some sort of zany road trip.

"Hey Rog Dog, how you doing on that game, Man," asked Harry.

"Good. I'm almost gettin' Homer and Bart back home." Roger replied without looking up.

"Go get your sister. I want to talk about something with the two of you."

When Roger turned around he noticed Myrlie. Then he ran off to retrieve his sister.

"Have a seat, Myrlie," Harry said. "Do you want anything to drink?" There was still lingering anger and hurt towards his mother but Harry decided that rudeness took more effort that civility. Myrlie shook her head no.

Several minutes later Harry's children, Marissa and Roger, returned to the den. Kristin was with them.

Myrlie was sitting on the couch. Her legs were crossed at the ankle. Her hands were folded in her lap.

"Sit down, kids," Harry said to his children. "You too, Kristin. Since you're going to be here, this is going to affect you too. Then he sat in one of the matching reclining chairs.

"You two have probably wondered about my family through the years. I know that you used to ask questions when you were younger and I can't even remember what I told you." The children were looking back and forth from Harry to Myrlie.

"Well, this lady here is my mother. Her name is Myrlie. This week is the first time that I've seen her in a very long time; the first time I've had a conversation with her in years. She found out about you and your mother for the first time this week. I have two brothers and a sister. I haven't seen them either in a long time. My mother wanted to meet her grandchildren. So that explains why I've been a little strange for the past few days. I've reunited with my mother."

Silence filled the room. Then Roger spoke.

"So, this is our other grandma? Hi, Grandma." Roger got up and hugged Myrlie. Marissa acknowledged Myrlie with a quick sideways glance. Then she walked over to father and kissed him on the cheek.

"Ready to kick some butt at that softball game, Princess." said Harry. "Let's bounce."

Myrlie was silent during the visit at their home. When they stopped for McDonald's at the children's request, she ordered a Big Mac with extra sauce, large fries and a large drink. She ate every bit of it. Harry thought that many women would envy her metabolism.

For dinner after the softball game, Harry, the kids and Myrlie went to the Rustic Inn seafood restaurant and ate crabs. Myrlie complimented Marissa. "You showed off out there, Girl. Glad I was there to see yo' team win." Marissa acted as if she wasn't there.

Roger had reenacted something silly he had seen Corey doing on *That's So Raven,* which lightened the mood. Marissa did not laugh. Every few minutes she would give Myrlie a glare that would melt ice. Harry wondered if Kristin had any inkling what she was getting herself into when she got involved with the Martin family.

After they returned Myrlie to the hotel Harry and the kids went to the Boomers Arcade. They had a blast, riding the bumper cars, bumper boats and playing video games. The kids screamed with excitement and terror on the roller coaster. Harry was happy to see that he and his children were responsible for putting a smile on Kristin's face. He had also been an unhappy child at one time.

Throughout the day at the barbecue on Sunday, Harry watched his children and their friends swimming, diving and splashing water on each other. More people stopped by than he had anticipated. He did not inform Myrlie of the event.

Joy came with her husband and twin daughters. The twins adored Marissa (the feeling was mutual). The twins' brownish curly hair flopped up and down as they trailed Marissa around the house. "Wia, Wia, Wook,Wook!" (Rissa, Rissa, Look, Look) the twins squealed. Marissa, Kristin, Tad and all the teenagers cracked up as the twins attempted cartwheels and flips. The teenagers laughed harder when the twins danced.

Everyone laughed and was on edge when Roy mimicked Usher's moves during the song "Yeah." Roy nearly fell over during the Michael Jackson/Jackson Five medley ("Smooth Criminal," "Beat It," "ABC," "I Want You Back"). Roger, Tommy, Monica's kids and Roy played Twister. The children laughed and moaned when Roy fell on them.

The adults played Poker, Bid Whist and Spades.

Roy had brought over his karaoke machine loaded up with almost any tune one could imagine. Roy sang off key versions of Kenny Chesney's "I Go Back," the Chilites' "Ooh Child," the Monkees' "Daydream Believer" Bob Dylan's "The Times They Are a Changing,"

Stevie Wonder's "For Once in My Life" and Michael Jackson's "Man in the Mirror."

David sang Al Green's "Let's Stay Together," Jeff Buckley's "Hallelujah" and the Beatles' "In My Life" and "Yesterday."

Marissa, Kristin and a friend Jasmine rocked Destiny Child's "Independent Women," Avril Lavinge's "Girlfriend," "Queen Latifah's "Just Another Day" and Rihanna's "Umbrella."

Dom and his wife Ramona performed duets of "Baby it's Cold Outside" by Ray Charles and Betty Carter, Frank Sinatra's "Fly Me to the Moon" and "Livin' on a Prayer" by Bon Jovi. Tori, Joy and Claire joined in on that song. Ramona sang sultry versions of Pat Benatar's songs "Hit Me with Your Best Shot" and "Heartbreaker."

Mrs. Appelbaum crooned Doris Day's "Que Sera Sera" and Perry Como's (and South Pacific's) "Some Enchanted Evening."

Sharon, Claire, Joy and Tori sang Cindy Lauper's "Girls Just Want to Have Fun." They also sang "I'm Every Woman" by Whitney Houston, "Respect" by Aretha Franklin and "Man! I Feel Like a Woman" by Shania Twain.

Mr. Gordon belted out "Life is a Song Worth Singing" by Teddy Pendergrass, Bette Midler's song "Wind Beneath My Wings," "In the Ghetto" by Elvis Presley, "Wild Horses" by the Rolling Stones and "Wake Up Everybody" by Harold Melvin & the Bluenotes. Harry had forgotten how well Mr. Gordon sang.

Delilah sang Led Zeppelin's "Stairway to Heaven," Alicia Keys'"I Know Why the Caged Bird Sings," Nirvana's "Smells Like Teen Spirit," Journey's "Don't Stop Believing" and "Somewhere Over the Rainbow."

Roger and Tommy giggled through New Edition's "Cool it Now" and "Candy Girl," and Sean Kingston's "Beautiful Girls."

Nora surprised everyone with touching, beautifully sung versions of "Because of You " by Kelly Clarkson, Pink's "Family Portrait," Fantasia's "I Believe," Carrie Underwood's "Lessons Learned," and "Mary J. Blige's "No More Drama." Her performances left everyone speechless because Nora hardly ever said a word.

Tori sang Barbra Streisand's song "People." Then she rocked Alannis Morisette's "Ironic" and brought down the house with Anita Baker's song "No One in the World." She and Roy performed duets of "The Beat Goes On" by Sonny and Cher and "Your Precious Love" by Marvin Gaye and Tammi Terrell. Tori did a Madonna medley including

"True Blue," "Little Star," "Get Into the Groove," and "My Baby's Got a Secret." She'd been Madonna's fan for years – had all sorts of Madonna memorabilia (records, photos, etc.). There were photos of Tori from the 80s dressed like Madonna in tulles skirts, bustiers, fishnet stockings, fingerless lace gloves and beads around her neck. Tori had also been a fan of Salt and Pepa.

Tori's final songs during the party were the Counting Crows' "Colorblind,"Jann Arden's "In Your Keeping," Eva Cassidy's "Songbird," and Tuck and Patti's "Take My Breath Away." Tori looked into Roy's eyes during those mellow performances. Sharon accompanied Tori on guitar during those last tunes.

Travis and Kristin individually freestyle rapped very personal, revealing rhymes. Their verses were witty, well done and poignant. Harry shook his head in amazement and pride as he observed the smooth, handsome, rapping doctor. Dr. Travis Smith's hair was in neat dreadlocks. Harry marveled at the former foul mouthed ten-year old.

Kristin once figuratively talked a million miles a minute and used to have a constant, infectious giggle. She was showing some of her old spark. Harry would have never thought so but he missed old Kristin. He knew it took time for some things to heal. Sometimes they never healed but he knew if the right kinds of people came into a person's life, they could help a person feel a whole lot better.

One moment Harry stood alone and stared at the dark evening sky. Tad joined him.

"My dad said you'd go with me to the *Star Trek* Convention," Tad said. "Some people don't care for stuff like that. You do. Thanks."

"No, problem," Harry replied. "Looking forward to it. Thanks for thinking of me. You're right - I do enjoy those types of events. Thanks for being a friend to Marissa." He patted Tad on the back.

Harry pointed to the sky, the moon and stars. The sky was velvety and lush. It was a mesmerizing cobalt-like shade of blue. The stars and moon were dazzling.

"Isn't all of this amazing?" Harry said.

"Yep," replied Tad.

The barbecue ended close to 11 p.m. After the guests had departed; after everything had been cleaned up and put away; and after everyone in the house had gone to bed, Harry went to sleep. That night he curled his body around his wife. He slept like a baby.

Chapter 20

Harry returned to work Monday morning. Rosita returned as well. His day was full with meetings. Dimaio and Martin's clients included people from a number of social class levels. There were wealthy men who wore expensive suits, carried leather briefcases and smelled of smooth, sweet, masculine colognes. These clients were billed at no less than $300.00 per hour. The firm's wealthier clients included high-class real estate people and developers, banking executives and several celebrities (who could be seen dressed in baggy pants and feathery sequined clothing). Then there were their mid-level clients – small business owners - men with their company's name as well as their own first names embroidered on their shirts. Their fees were determined on a case-by-case basis.

Finally, there were those people who were able to pay a very minimal fee or no fee at all. On this Monday, many of Harry's pro bono clients who had been on hold the previous week streamed in and out. Rosita and Felicia took care of those clients whose matter could be handled by telephone calls or letter with an attorney's signature.

Some people could not read or read very little and were unable to comprehend the contents of a letter. The secretaries helped with that. If the clients need something that required intervention from an attorney, they could speak with Harry. It was amazing how quickly some situations could be resolved through a phone call or letter from an attorney's office.

Cases involving certain types of ongoing litigation were transferred to lawyers who worked on contingency. The firm did not specialize in personal injury cases. If it were a complicated social service issue, the client would be referred to either Mr. Gordon or other appropriate agencies. The secretaries were well-compensated for their extra duties and were constantly told to inform Harry or Dom if they felt too overloaded.

Sometimes Dom would walk in and sigh. "Good grief, what in the hell are we running here, a social service agency or a law firm?" In the lounge there was a couch and usually coffee, tea, muffins, doughnuts and bagels that were brought in by a woman named Heather. She ran a small business in which she delivered breakfast products to companies in the building.

Some of the firm's visitors would seem so relaxed one would think they were at their home. Dom was a nosy, friendly sort of fellow and would sometimes sit in the lobby to listen to some of the conversations that were taking place. Some conversations could be a rather tawdry and intriguing, with people discussing tales of sex, affairs, feuds, etc. Since Dimaio and Martin was not a criminal law firm, these outside cases provided the thrill and intrigue that was often missing in the corporate arena. Many of these people were unemployed so they had nowhere else to be. Some had to be gently escorted out of the office when they overstayed their visit.

That Monday Dom ended up assisting with the overflow of indigent guests. Deli sandwiches were ordered and delivered to the office.

Harry could no longer remember the first time Rosita and Felicia requested assistance for someone they knew. The word of mouth advertising made them become busier by the day. He and Dom had already decided that it was time to hire another attorney and had advertised at the area's law schools.

Harry's long day at work had winded him up. He called home to see if the family was in the mood for hanging out. The kids and Mrs. Appelbaum passed on the invitation. Mrs. Appelbaum did not want to miss *Dancing with the Stars*. The kids wanted to order pizza. They had school the following morning.

When Claire showed up at Harry's office, she was wearing a long, clingy red fishtail skirt with a slit on one side and a matching top that fit snugly against her skin. (The outfit was designed by Delilah and made by Nora). On Claire's feet were sandals with low heels and straps that wrapped around her ankles. She wore diamond studs in her ears.

Harry said "Dayum, you look good!" when he laid eyes on her.

Claire and Harry ate dinner at an upscale Chinese restaurant on South Beach. After eating they strolled along Lincoln Street. They heard someone yelling.

"Harry! Harry Martin!"

A short, round woman was walking quickly towards them carrying a huge multi-colored flowered tote bag. She was dressed in a flowery peasant skirt and purple turtleneck sweater. Her eyeglass frames were huge round circles with red rims. She was waving one hand frantically. Silver bangles clanged as they hit each other while slipping down the woman's arm.

"Wow!" Harry shouted. He realized who it was.

"Harry? Harry Martin! Oh, my goodness. Well I'll be. It *is* Harry Martin!" The short woman grabbed Harry in a tight bear hug and then stood back.

"Harry, it's me, Ms. O'Donnell, but since you're no longer my student, you may call me Gabby. Short for Gabrielle. I know it's been ages but I never forget my favorite students. And is this your wife? Are you still acting? Does she know that you were one smashing Othello? Or fantastic as Tom in *The Glass Menagerie*. I haven't been teaching for over ten years. Until recently, I've been performing off Broadway. Now, I've hit the big time. I'm portraying the Evil Witch from the West in the *Wizard of Oz*. We've been going around the whole country and the tickets are selling out like hot cakes - in one day in some places. It's grueling work but it's been a fantastic opportunity."

"Harry, so how are you? You disappeared on me after high school." She hugged him again. She touched his face. She hugged Claire, who was taken aback.

"I'm doing fine Mrs. O'Donnell," Harry said. "It's good to see you! It's real good to see you! It's been a long time. Wow!" Tears unexpectedly came into Harry's eyes.

Harry hadn't thought about Ms. O'Donnell in years. With Ms. O'Donnell and Mr. Gordon's help, Harry managed to attend the same high school for four years and graduate with honors. Back then, she had curly brown hair, freckles and chipmunk like cheeks. She was not much older than her students were. During high school Mrs. O'Donnell kept track of Harry no matter where he was. In her purple VW Beetle she transported him to and from his "homes" to their productions. She drove fast, spoke rapidly and a lot. Harry would have to hang on to dear life when Ms. O'Donnell made quick turns on the road.

"Claire, this is Ms. O'Donnell. Ms. O'Donnell, this is my wife Claire. Ms. O'Donnell was my English teacher and drama coach. She stuck with me all through high school. She found me in every place I lived. Ms. O'Donnell, do you still have that purple VW. I don't think I ever got the chance to thank you back then. Thanks for everything, Ms. O'Donnell." He could feel a lump growing in his throat,

"No, I had to put ole Sally down. That car did last several years, though. Harry, do you have children? Please come see my show this week. I will leave tickets for your family at the ticket booth. They're very difficult to obtain. She dug in her purse, scrambled around, and found a note pad. Here's my phone number. Call me. We'll catch up after the show. Right now, I'm on my way to meet friends. You look wonderful Harry. Nice meeting you, Claire." She squeezed his hand, hugged them both and swiftly walked away.

Harry avoided Claire's eyes as they drove back to his office building to retrieve his car. He was unable to bear witness to the shock he was sure was in her eyes. He had been holding another secret – he had been an actor, a thespian. Not just in real life, but on the stage as well.

Chapter 21

Claire was dumbfounded. It seemed as if everyday she was learning something new about her husband. Now, here was this woman who talked a million miles a minute bragging about what a wonderful actor Harry was. As they drove back to retrieve Harry's car from the parking garage, she couldn't think of anything to say. Her mother would have not believed it. Claire Martin was speechless.

Chapter 22

It was Wednesday night – now a week and several hours from the day that Myrlie arrived. To placate Mrylie and keep peace, they extended Myrlie's hotel stay for an additional week, which would take her up to Wednesday morning of the following week. On Tuesday, Harry hired a courier to deliver a postal money order to Myrlie at the hotel. The money order was enough or would have to be enough spending money to last Myrlie for the week. It was one way to keep her quiet and out of their hair. Tuesday had gone without much excitement. The family had eaten a meal of meat loaf, mashed potatoes and sweet peas – a normal American family meal.

Chapter 23

Although the Wednesday showing of the play occurred on a school night the Martin family as well as Mrs. Appelbaum, Kristin, Nora and Delilah, attended the *Wizard of Oz* on Broadway. Prior to the show the family and their guests had eaten at Michy's, a pleasant, eclectic restaurant that served Latin and Mediterranean comfort foods with a gourmet twist. Claire hoped that there would no battles when it was time for the children to wake up the following morning for school.

Delilah had pleaded with Claire for an invitation. "You've gotta take me with you," Delilah begged. "I've been dying to see this show! The tickets sell out often in a day. Claire, I'll do anything for you – let me go." Harry had contacted Ms. O'Donnell and requested tickets for Delilah and Nora. It worked out that they were all able to sit together.

Ms. O'Donnell was excellent as the Evil Witch of the West. She was scary and her appearance was completely transformed with green body paint and warts. Claire thought that the show was great, keeping basically true to the original movie, but additional features were added that made the show more current with today's culture. There was more diversity in the cast. Dorothy was a played by a stunning Asian actress who had a singing voice that reached several high octaves. Claire's mother had been a fan of the original Dorothy, Judy Garland. The Cowardly lion was portrayed by a funny black guy. "Oh, Man, Man, Man," he'd cry when they encountered a precarious situation.

The tin man was a brawny Hispanic dude whose face and hands were spray-painted silver. He wore a silver costume. The muscular baritone managed to evoke sympathy from the audience every time he cried "Ay Carumba" when his "metal" body began to stiffen up. He delivered some of his lines in a form of Spanglish,

A thin white guy with strawberry blonde curly hair played the scarecrow. He delivered a rapid rap solo about what he'd do if he only had a brain. His body was quite flexible and he was very convincing every time he stumbled to the ground.

Glinda, the Good Witch from the North was portrayed by a beautiful black woman with mahogany hued skin. She was dressed in a shimmery satin, tulles topped pink-hooped gown with sheer puffy sleeves.

114

The Wizard was a tall, debonair, dark haired tenor and actor (Robert Goulet or Engelbert Humperdinck type) who completely gave himself to the role that was presented as an absent minded professor type character.

Some of the songs from the original movie were used and pumped up by the live orchestra and vocalists. There were also several new tunes. The Follow the Yellow Brick road scene included exhilarating music and dancing, with ballet, acrobatics, pop locking and break dancing. A fantastic bongo player performed with the orchestra.

After the show the Martins and their friends met Ms. O'Donnell backstage. Ms. O'Donnell talked up a storm.

"Well, what did you all think? Did you enjoy it? Harry, does this make you think about doing stage work again?" She didn't give anyone time to answer her questions. "Please wait for me while I change out of my costume and remove this makeup." When she returned she was wearing lime green harem styled pants and a blue beaded top with puffy sleeves.

"Ms. O'Donnell," said Harry. "We're going to get dessert. Come with us, please. My treat."

Ms. O'Donnell started rambling minutes after they were seated at the restaurant. "Well, Harry," she said. "It appears that everything has turned our all right for you. I was in contact with Mr. Gordon for a couple of years so I knew that you had begun attending college. You were a very intelligent young man. What do you do for work now?"

Since Harry couldn't get a chance to speak, he handed Ms. O'Donnell one of his business cards that read: *Harry Martin, PA., Dimaio and Martin, Attorneys at Law. A* waiter appeared and took their orders.

"You are a lawyer. Good for you, Harry!" Ms. O'Donnell exclaimed. "Kids, did you know that your dad was a wonderful actor? And to me he was so special. Mrs. O'Donnell teared up. Harry, I was sad that I never got a chance to tell you goodbye. Oh, my goodness, Harry. You were such a special young man. Back then, I wasn't much older then you all, my students. I was still in my early twenties. You were so thoughtful.

"There was a time when it seemed as if my whole life was crashing in around me. I had broken up with my boyfriend, a guy that I can now see wasn't worth much, but back then I was crushed. My grandfather, whom I was extremely close to, had begun acting strangely, disappearing and forgetting who we, his family members, were. Now we know that he had been suffering from Alzheimer's.

"All of my problems came to a head one weekend. My grandfather had been missing for three days and we'd finally found him on a Sunday. He was dehydrated and disoriented and we were forced to hospitalize him. So, I had broken up with my boyfriend and was stressed about my grandfather. I was severely depressed and on the verge of a nervous breakdown. I was tempted to quit my job and just lock myself up in my apartment. I went through several boxes of Kleenex that weekend. I was a wreck. I decided to go to work. Harry, your husband, your dad," she said, glancing around the dining table, "had moved into another place. He hadn't figured out the bus routes yet. Harry needed a ride to school that Monday."

There was a brief interlude in Ms. O'Donnell's story when the waiter brought their food. Once everyone had received his or her food, Ms. O'Donnell started up again. "Now, where was I? Oh, yes. Well, Harry rarely talked much, but on that Monday, I truly believe he saved my life. I had not discussed anything with Harry about my troubles, but when Harry got into my car, he handed me a vase with flowers he had picked. Gorgeous, beautiful flowers. He handed me a thank you card, saying he appreciated everything I'd done for him. He made me laugh, reading some corny jokes that were on some candy wrappers. That day I would look up and see Harry glancing into my classroom door between his classes checking up on me. When I dropped him off to his home, he gently squeezed my hand before exiting the car.

"Every day that week Harry gave me something; one day it was a pair of earrings, another day it was a stuffed animal. He must have used his allowance money. Later it dawned on me that the stresses of my life must have been taking a toll on me before that week and were evident to anyone looking at me. Of course, I had been fighting with my boyfriend for a long time. I had been worried about my grandfather for months. This boy, now this man, Harry, saw my pain. There were other occasions when Harry, probably unaware, came through for me. This kid who had problems of his own was concerned about me.

"Harry was in one of the English classes during my first year of teaching. I've always loved Shakespeare, drama, poetry, all of that stuff and had decided to take on the drama coach position at the school. I noticed Harry's oratory talents for the first time when he recited

Rudyard Kipling's *If*. This young man, who used to sit almost completely silent in my class, had this amazing soulful manner of reading poetry and drama. I begged and pleaded with him to join the school's drama team. He was wonderful. I started learning of his difficult life when I began giving him rides home. One evening he and I stayed late to clean up after a performance. I saw him waiting for a bus and offered him a ride home. It sort of became my habit to transport him back and forth to school. He was great company for me.

"Wow, Harry, there were quite a few places we've seen. I remember overhearing one kid announce to Harry, "Hey, Dude, there's some weird lookin' white lady waitin' for you.' I've always been somewhat funky in my clothing choices. I know that. When days went by and I hadn't heard from Harry, I'd contact Harry's old social worker, Mr. Gordon. Harry used to talk about him all the time and I found out who and where he was. We even communicated for a short time after he moved here to Miami. Harry, are still close to Mr. Gordon?" Harry nodded.

Mrs. O'Donnell took a deep breath. Then she said, "It's great to see you Harry. Let's not ever lose touch again."

There was silence following Ms. O'Donnell's story. The silence was shattered when Roger went into a recitation of a sexually innuendo filled conversation between Jake and Charlie on the TV show *Two and A Half Men*.

"And then Jake said _____," announced Roger. "And then Charlie said _____. Man, those dudes crack me up. Ma, how 'bout that time when Charlie and Alan's momma got that botox stuff in her lips? Hoo, that was funny!"

There was giggling around the table as well as some embarrassment. *Two and Half Men* was sort of a family show, yet it could be a little risqué. At ten, Roger really did not have a complete grasp on the dialogue he was repeating. The boy who played Jake probably didn't get all of the jokes either. Claire thought they could be probably monitor Roger's television viewing habits a little closer, but Claire really did love her some Evelyn Harper. Just thinking about Evelyn walking around with her lips all puffed up made Claire almost erupt into hysterical laughter, but with some effort, she managed to hold it down.

Claire spoke softly to her husband later that evening.

"Baby, I cannot believe the past of week," she quietly said. "I've probably learned more about you these last few days than I've known over all these years. Harry has a family, Harry was an actor. Promise me, sweetheart. If there's ever anything that's bothering you, you'll come talk to me. Let me there for you. Let me love you like you deserve to be loved. Okay, Harry?"

"I promise baby," Harry whispered.

Then they made sweet love.

Chapter 24

Myrlie's stay in Miami lastcd a little over a month. After the second week at the Marriott, Harry allowed Myrlie to move in and sleep in the family guest room. Myrlie and Roger developed some sort of bond. Roger was a very forgiving soul. Harry refrained himself when he arrived home one day and saw Myrlie playing a game of *Uno* with Roger. People could be different with their grandchildren. Seeing them interact encouraged Harry to resume family game night in the home with *Checkers, Trouble, Connect Four* and other games. Mrylie escorted Roger and Tommy for trick or treating on Halloween night. She wore black tights, a black leotard, a pink tutu-like skirt and cat ears. She drew cat whiskers on her face. Roger and Tommy were Ninjas. Later that night, a wary Harry questioned Roger about Myrlie's words and actions. He was satisfied with Roger's reponses. It appeared that Myrlie had not mistreated his son.

Marissa was cordial but Harry felt that she knew that there was some serious history between Myrlie and him. She was apparently withholding judgment. Claire followed Harry's lead. She'd decided that Myrlie's place in their lives would be Harry's decision. Mrs. Appelbaum, after ensuring that it was okay with Harry, invited Myrlie to join her at some of her senior classes. Dom met Myrlie – he visited the house on a suspiciously vague reason. Myrlie's outfit that day surely had to pique his interest even more. She was dressed in neon pink leggings, a satiny pink off the shoulder satin dress and opened toed, opened back stilettos with pink feathers. She had on a blonde wig that was straight with bangs that came down across her forehead.

Myrlie's departure date was her choice. One day she announced that she was going to visit a friend of hers in DC. There had been no discussion about whether or not or when she would return to Miami. Harry had never gotten around to discussing the reasons for her anger and why she had abused her children.

A couple of weeks after Myrlie's departure there was a bash at the Martin home. Even though the barbecue turned out to be a great day of socializing, Harry thought that it would be nice to have another festive evening with the special people in his life. He conferred with

Claire and they decided to have the celebration. Luvey's restaurant catered the occasion.

The guests included Nora and Juno (who were apparently dating – shocking news to Claire). Delilah was there with her female partner Sue Fong. Also attending the party were Dom and his wife Ramona; Mr and Mrs. Dimaio; Rosita, Rosita's husband; and Felicia and Felicia's boyfriend. Mr. Gordon and his wife Harriett were at the party. The Gordons' children (now adults), Benji and Emma, stopped by for several minutes. Travis came with his wife, Tanya, and their son, Sean.

Harry and Dom's eyes met when Aunt Stella arrived in a tight tiger print dress and tiger print mule shoes. During the party, Roger and his friends, plus Sean and Monica's children, ran throughout the house and the backyard. Claire's friends Tori, Joy and Sharon and their partners were at the party. Joy's twins stayed close to Marissa. Marissa and her friends cracked up over the little girls' antics.

Mrs. Appelbaum and her friend Sadie had dates – two men they knew from the senior center. Harry discreetly gave Mrs. Appelbaum a thumbs up. Ms. O'Donnell was there with a man who looked old enough to be her father. Rodolfo, the dance teacher, made an appearance.

There was a lot of dancing, laughing and hugging at the party. Roy Johnson served as DJ at the party and the music kept the guests on their feet. Harry couldn't resist having Roy play the Beegees' *Night Fever* to get Uncle Rico going. Sure enough, Uncle Rico, dresssed in a polyester, sky blue suit, was on his feet disco dancing. Dom raised his wine glass and winked at Harry.

Claire, Marissa, Kristin and a few of Marissa's other friends gave lessons to Mrs. Dimaio when the guests danced the *Electric Slide*, *Cha Cha* and other modern line dances. The *Macarena, YMCA, Chicken Dance* were also danced at the party. There was a *Soul Train* line. Other dance music included "Shout" by Isley Brothers, Bruce Springsteen's "Dancing in the Dark," Freddie Jackson's "Jam Tonight," the Doobie Brothers "China Grove," Justin Timberlake's "Rock Your Body," Kool and the Gang's "Get Down On It," Luther Vandross' "Bad Boy/Having a Party," "Groove Tonight" by Earth Wind and Fire and other songs

Claire requested "Give You My Heart," by Babyface and Toni Braxton, "Best of My Love" by the Emotions, "I'm in Luv" by Joe Thomas and "Back in Stride" by Frankie Beverly and Maze. She grabbed Harry's hand and they danced. Mr. and Mrs. Martin grooved to "I Knew I Loved You" by Savage Garden, "All I Want Is Forever," by Regina Belle and J.T. Taylor, and "Lost Without You" by Robin Thicke   Those were a few of Harry's favorite songs. During "(I've Had) The Time Of My Life," Harry and Claire held each other and laughed. Their life together had come full circle.

The Sisteristas gave their first live performance at the party, performing some of Tori's old, now updated and revised songs, as well as some of Joy's compositions. With a little more practice, Harry thought they would be ready for a real audience very soon.

The party ran late into the night and after everyone left, Harry and Claire danced to their own "Slow Jam Urban" mix (music by Jaheim, Joe Thomas, Jagged Edge, New Edition, Donnell Jones, Jodeci, Troop, Mint Condition and Boyz II Men). Unnoticed by either Claire of Harry was their daughter Marissa peeking around the edge of a wall observing her parents. For about ten minutes, Marissa quietly watched her parents dance and look into each other's eyes. She nodded her head, contentedly smiled, and then went to bed.

It did not take long for the couple to get in the mood for some lovemaking, getting through just a small portion of their music mix. The evening came to a close in Harry and Claire's king sized bed.

Chapter 25

Harry began to search the Internet for his brothers and sister. The search became a project that he and Marissa worked on together. Harry also hired private investigators to help him locate his siblings. Marissa and Roger were fascinated by the idea of having more family out there. Harry was considering learning more about his biological father, Hammer (as called by Myrlie). Myrlie said Hammer's real name was Sylvester Davis.

Rebecca's harassment of Roger ended shortly after Roger reported Rebecca's antics to her father when the dad dropped Rebecca off to school one day.

Harry and Delilah had formed a friendship. With the revelation that they had shared similar childhoods, there was a special bond between the two of them. The young woman had found someone who could relate to what she had been though in the foster care system. She was in a difficult period of deciding whether she wanted to have a relationship with her own biological parents. She was beginning to feel her father did the best he could. Delilah revealed that her mother had located her and was trying to start a relationship. Delilah was unsure if she would ever allow that to happen.

An additional bed was placed in Marissa's room for Kristin. The Martins did not want Kristin out on the street. They decided that they had room in their home and lives for the girl. Kristin had already received a brand new bed comforter with images of *Tweety's* face all over it from the Martins. Kristin's mother was planning to visit in a few months. Her mother had agreed to allow Kristin to stay with the Martins during her deployment.

Already Harry had heard bits of conversations regarding cute boys and giggling coming from Marissa's room. The sounds were music to his ears.

Harry and Dom decided that some restrictions be placed on the pro bono cases that were coming into the office. The number of walk-ins was becoming overwhelming for the secretaries. The attorneys decided that definite appointments should be scheduled for all of their clients, and that 10 hours per week would be allocated for the pro-bono clients.

Harry and Claire's relationship improved greatly and they grew closer during the months following Myrlie's visit. Harry and Claire began to talk more freely and honestly.

Myrlie's visit had opened up a past Harry had tried to forget, but he realized that he did not have to endure the painful memories alone. He was almost afraid to completely embrace the happiness and love that was currently in his life; that by doing so he would end up disappointed. He decided he was willing to take a chance. Harry felt that he was becoming a whole person. He was ready for the rest of his life to begin.